STOLEN BY THE SHEIKH

MOLLIE MATHEWS

Blue Orchid
PUBLISHING

STOLEN BY THE SHEIKH

THE SHEIKHS UNTAMED BRIDES

MOLLIE MATHEWS

"The wound is the place where the light enters."
~ *Rumi*

ABOUT THIS LOVE STORY

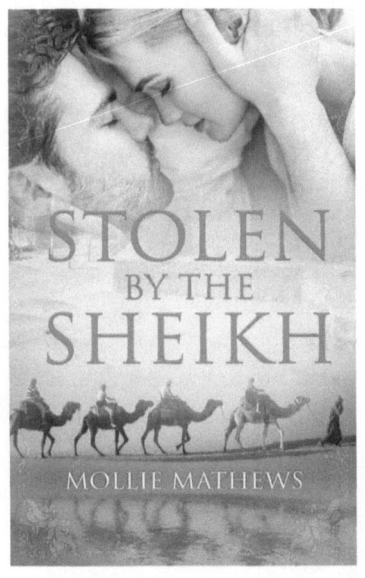

In life and love, it's never too late
for a second chance. . .
This is not one of those times.

Fiercely independent contemporary artist Lucy Ford was absolutely content with her life—until the day Anwar na Hassir strolled into her gallery and back into her life.

She had dreamed of being a mother and would soon have a son. Being a single mum wasn't the happy ending she had visualised, but at least she had someone to love. Someone of her own. Someone she could keep forever.

As long as the child's father never found out. Anwar could not, would not, must not ever know the truth. Not if she was to keep her child.

Anwar was as formidable as Lucy was freewheeling. Luring Lucy to his desert Kingdom, somewhere between the magic of the desert and the stroll along the ocean, she lets him steal her heart. Only to discover love, once given, can never be returned.

A sensuous tale of modern love, career-crossed relationships, the heady magic of instant attraction, loss, and the unwavering faith that sustains them—even in the darkest hour.

INCLUDES 3 BONUS CHAPTERS

Claimed By The Sheikh

If you love beautiful stories set against a sensuous backdrop of the sensuous desert, art and innovative architecture, you'll love *Claimed by The Sheikh*.

PRAISE FOR STOLEN BY THE SHEIKH

"I loved *Stolen By The Sheikh*! The depth of emotions of both going back to their childhoods and how they were raised touched my heart! Such a heartbreaking way to grow up. Both seemed to have worked their way through that and came out on top!! Best kind of story for sure! My kind of story!"

~5-Star Review

"This book is so worth the read. I was hooked from the very first page. I loved how talented and incredibly creative Lucy is. The obstacles and challenges are met with determination and courage. I loved all the twists and confidence these characters show. You won't be able to put this book down until you reach the last page."

~Loreli

"An exciting, sensual addition to the Sheikh romance genre. Thank you so much for writing this story."

"Stolen By The Sheik is beautiful. The world-building is so needed now, and the messages that you are highlighting are powerful. I will have to go and read some of your other books in this series/world."

"There is plenty of conflict…I wonder if they will ever get their happily ever after?"

"I enjoyed how the author was able to paint a picture of the characters' lives."

"At the end of chapter #3, I said to myself, is that all? I want to read more, I was so very engrossed."

"I think you have a winner with this book, it is very enjoyable."

"I enjoyed what I've read so far, I totally got into the story."

"I often wonder how authors come up with the stories they do. This one has a good premise."

"*Stolen By The Sheikh* drew me in with vibrant, colorful, and touching dialogue. I felt I got to know the characters and where they were coming from."

"Vivid descriptions, as well as wonderfully crafted words, elicit the feelings of the characters that I could embody."

"The prequel of *Stolen By The Sheikh* left me wanting to read the book in its entirety with the strength of the dialogue and depth of the characters and story."

CHAPTER ONE

T ruth? Where did anyone even begin? Sheikh Anwar na Hassir questioned. In a world enamored with lies, the truth seemed as impossible to extract as the rarest sapphire in his Ceylonese mines.

It begins with finding the woman who brought the curse of shame onto his family. Lucy Gaysford. Except she wasn't Lucy Gaysford anymore, he growled, reading the shortened name emblazoned across the gallery window, signaling the solo exhibition by artist Lucy Ford. Anwar wrapped the gold New Zealand Merino scarf tighter around his neck, stealing himself to New York's wintery bite as he stood outside the Manhattan art gallery and glanced in.

Lucy had been economical with the truth before. What other secrets was she now keeping?

Why had he come? In pursuit of truth and justice, he told himself, registering the kick of anticipation that trembled through his stomach as he caught a glimpse of his target. His eyes trailed her backless dress, revealing the sensual curve of her spine as she wove through the crowd. A jolt of longing quivered through him.

Beauty, that's all, he cursed, forcing forbidden desire to a dull, barely perceivable tremor. Dammit. Why couldn't he shake the longing, the need, the desire? Why couldn't he forget the pain of her betrayal?

Family honor came the answer. To find the truth no matter the cost. He clenched his fist, bending his formidable will to his purpose. He would force from her the confession that her escape from his kingdom had evaded. He would silence the uneasy sense that he had been mistaken. That it was his beloved brother who was the cause of so much hurt. But to believe that Hamad, his own flesh and blood, might've lied was untenable. Wasn't it better to accept the deceit of a Westerner, a woman with whom he had a short, passionate fling, rather than yield to the realization that his own family had betrayed his love?

He paused before joining the intoxicated crowd inside, liquored up with complimentary drinks designed to adle their minds and open their wallets. He turned and glanced at the snow-lined streets adorned with glitter and baubles for the festive season.

Thankfully, the gallery had not gone overboard with tawdry tinsel and garish, neon Christmas lights celebrating the birth of the Christian son his culture did not recognize but knew instead as God's prophet. As Anwar redirected his attention indoors, he noticed with admiration that both unsettled and pleased him that the gallery was a shrine to love.

Love! He mused, noticing discomfort prickle his skin. What did he know of love? Oh yes—love of the inanimate. That was his refuge. Art, nature, his prized exotic orchids, and Zephyr, his loyal falcon from whom he was rarely parted. These were the loves upon which he could rely.

He narrowed his formidable gaze in search of the woman

he was here to make atone for the sin of her betrayal. He would extract her confession and then be done with Lucy, *whatever her name was*, forever.

CHAPTER TWO

S he dreamed of dunes turning gold beneath the molten orange sun. She dreamed of bathing in the turquoise waters of the Persian Gulf. But most of all, she dreamed of him.

Barely conscious of the crowd pressing around her at the opening of her art exhibition, Lucy Ford's heart quickened as she scanned the painting on display by the door. Shining like a beacon, it attracted people struggling along the streets away from the wild winds and icy snow battering Manhattan's streets.

She had entitled it *Desert Dreams*. It was her favorite painting, created during the full moon three months earlier, 12 weeks after her heart was broken by Anwar na Hassir. Sheikh Anwar na Hassir, she corrected. The formidable, playboy bachelor whose baby she now carried.

The artwork had flowed from her in a symphony of colors born of anguish and joy. She still found it hard to believe that she had procured such an astonishing piece from her imagination.

Clutching the exhibition catalog to her chest, Lucy turned

from the painting and swept her gaze over the crowd crammed into the Manhattan art gallery. She tried to catch the attention of Issy Riley, the art therapist who had encouraged her to paint her way to healing. But Issy was deep in conversation with her husband, Massimiliano Balforni, CEO of Emporio Balforni. Lucy loved the easy way they were together and their deep love. She wished she could have a love like that. A love that weathered the fiercest storms. A love that lasted.

She placed her palm over the slight swell of her belly. Sometimes dreams do come true, she reminded herself. She had dreamed of being a mother and would soon have a son. Being a single mom wasn't the happy ending she had visualized, but at least she had someone to love. Someone of her own. Someone she could love forever.

As long as the child's father never found out. Anwar could never know the truth. Not if she was to keep her child.

"You have an admirer," the gallery owner, Maria Bright, said as she placed a round red sticker below Lucy's painting, *Desert Dreams*.

Conflicting feelings at the confirmed sale threaded through Lucy's heart. Regret at losing the artwork she had poured her soul into creating, laced with joy in knowing that someone loved the painting as much as she did. She had priced *Desert Dreams* ridiculously high in the hope of deterring a purchaser. It was special to her, and she wanted to keep it forever. But she had to face reality. She would soon be a single parent and needed the money. Whoever had bought *Desert Dreams* had deep pockets. *Very, very deep pockets.*

"Gosh, what a relief, Maria. Imagine if none of my paintings had sold, and I couldn't repay your kindness. I hope the commission covers all your costs," Lucy said.

Maria grinned. "It's a fabulous result for both of us."

"I'm so grateful. You took a gamble on me with this solo exhibition. Without you, I never would have had the courage to show my paintings."

"Darling, I adore your work. And so does your new collector. Come and meet him, Lucy. He is quite obsessed with you."

"With me?" Lucy asked as she wove her way through the crowd. "Or with my paintings?"

"Both," Maria said, coming to a halt beside the tall, dark, dazzling man Lucy had glimpsed from behind earlier. "Your Royal Highness, let me introduce you to the artist."

"Anwar!" His name clung to her dry mouth.

"Lucy." The scorching look he gave her was reserved for Lucy and Lucy alone.

Maria's eyebrows lifted as her mouth gaped open. "*You know each other?*"

His heated gaze blatantly acknowledged the night he still remembered and the past Lucy would rather forget.

A barely perceivable tug lifted the corners of Maria's lips. "I'll leave you to get reacquainted."

Lucy's face blazed with heat. She steadfastly avoided Anwar's gaze and fixed her eyes on the back of Maria's glossy hair as she drifted back into the crowd.

"You've been hiding from me." His deep, velvet voice held the trace of the Middle Eastern accent that had weakened her willpower six months before. She had steeled her resolve never to be moved by Anwar should their paths cross again. As that control slipped from her, panic buzzed through her chest.

The catalog she'd clenched in her hands fluttered to the floor. She stooped to pick it up as he lowered his powerful frame to retrieve the booklet showcasing her collection. As she lifted her gaze to Anwar's face, his dark amber eyes magnetically pulled hers to his as he waited for her response.

For a stomach-clenching moment, she thought he knew the truth. "Hiding?" she stuttered.

"Your talent."

Lucy exhaled in a whoosh of relief.

"You kept it a secret from me. Why?"

How could she tell him because she didn't believe in herself? All her life, her narcissistic mother had told her to aim small. She'd been told repeatedly not to outshine her brothers and sisters. She felt her throat constrict. All those silent protests she'd swallowed congealed on her tongue. How could she speak to them now?

"I'm in awe."

She so badly wanted to feel nothing but hatred for the man who had betrayed her so mercilessly. Hatred would steel her resolve. Hatred would keep her lips sealed. Hatred would keep her safe. But the sonorous tone of his praise made Lucy's body flame with heat, sending a tell-tale crimson blush to her cheeks. It wasn't the memory of that sensual, sexy night when their son had been conceived nor the compliment he offered now. It was how his voice resonated with every scarred artery in her heart, awakening the lingering dream of a happily-ever-after that refused to die.

Her eyes trailed the length of his 6-foot two-inch frame, then rose to his face. The curated gallery lights spotlighted the starkly molded framework of his features. He still exuded the authority and compelling magnetism that sent her pulse soaring and her willpower plummeting.

Damn it!

She should never have slept with him. But now, at least, she knew the truth. She was just another conquest in an endless sea of women. Common. Plentiful. Replaceable. As easy to possess as the seams of sapphire in his Ceylonese mines, the abundant priceless pearls beneath the sea surrounding his desert kingdom, and rich oil reserves that were readily replenished. For a man of his considerable wealth, nothing was priceless. *Not even love.*

Heat, longing, and fury shot through her loins as her awareness returned to the absurdly handsome sheikh who must never know he had fathered her child. Lucy shifted her gaze to Issy and Max, hoping to catch their attention and give her a reason to escape the awkward situation she now found herself in.

"How did you find me?"

"I was passing through."

"New York?" she challenged disbelievingly.

Anwar turned and fixed his gaze momentarily on the stark white wall closest to the door. On the white panel was her name in gold letters, *Lucy Ford*, and the show's title, *Desert Dreams*.

"This is a solo exhibition, and you are the star. I was curious. What were these desert dreams, and who was having them?"

Lucy studied a splash of red wine puddling on the floor. She grimaced as her face blazed with heat. She wanted to say, 'The desert dreams were those you promised me when you took my virginity. The desert dreams you stole when you abandoned me. The desert dreams I now carry.' But she would not share her wound and dignify the hurt he had inflicted. Nor would he ever know her secret.

"Your paintings, you've captured the emotion exactly."

"You're being kind," Lucy said, steeling her heart to his praise. Why was he flattering her? Her rational mind rallied to protect her. Don't let your guard down. Not again. He can't be trusted.

"The desolation. The loneliness. The isolation. But you've taken it further. You've seen the hope, healing, and beauty below the surface. The desert is not a barren wilderness. It dances with life. With dreams," he corrected.

His gaze shifted from her to the painting he had just purchased, running along the soaring dunes troughed on the canvas with a hurtle of ochre and lashings of gold. Then his eyes rose along the formidable shaft of light that Lucy had painted with an intuitive blaze of gold, its beam towering over the dunes like a protective benefactor.

"You have a rare ability to capture feelings," he said, turning to her again. Dark amber eyes, deep and solid as crystal, held her spellbound. "I knew you had to be mine."

"You had your chance."

He laughed, the easy laugh that only those with supreme confidence exuded. "What I meant was, I knew I had to make your paintings mine."

She grimaced. There he was, rejecting her again. "We don't need you," she tossed at him, regretting the comment immediately. "I don't need you," she hastily corrected.

A flicker of confusion quirked his brows, and then he gestured toward *Desert Dreams*. "I fell in love with it the first time I saw it. I don't know why…it speaks to me, somehow."

It should, Lucy thought to herself. *It's about us*. Now, the title seemed too obvious. Too foolish. Too dangerous. Lucy's breath caught in her chest as her thoughts returned to that fateful night that inspired the painting.

Escaping into her art had soothed her soul and her pain. And for some reason, she was glad Anwar was now the new owner. One day, she would tell her son about their love story. Her child would never know he was unwanted. She would protect him from that hurt. The love with which he was conceived was embodied in the painting. As for Anwar? She felt nothing.

Worry wormed through her gut as she registered the lie. She prayed inwardly that Anwar would be content to add her paintings to his already formidable art collection and that their paths would never cross again.

"The painting evokes such strong feelings," he said. "There's something about the whole collection. Something deliciously familiar."

She shuddered as she caught the dangerous glint dancing in his eyes.

"What am I missing?"

Lucy shook her head, sending a curtain of glossy blonde hair sweeping across her shoulders. "Nothing. They're landscapes from my mind. Dreams. That's all. I wouldn't read too much into them."

"Dreams," he repeated. "The feeling that one has been reborn."

A gaze of silent understanding united them, muting the noise and clatter of the crowd. She felt suddenly adrift, like sand in a storm. A reckless desire to confess the truth rose from her belly. "Anwar, there's something—"

"Lucy, another collector, Grace Hunt, Executive Chairwoman of Ferrari, would like to meet you," Maria said, rushing to her side before the truth could be revealed. "Grace is also a trustee of MoMA. She adores your series and insists I introduce you. If I may steal Lucy away, Your Royal Highness?" Maria added apologetically.

The ill-timed request temporarily shattered their sacred union. Perhaps it was just as well. Anwar and she had a flawed history. He had proven he was unreasonable, unpredictable, and unreliable. It would be naive and foolish to trust that he would do the right thing by her when he discovered she was carrying his son. *His firstborn child. His heir.*

"Wait!" Anwar said suddenly, with an air of explosive command. "I'll buy them all."

"*The paintings?*" Maria asked. "*All of them?*"

Lucy's pulse rate ricocheted as Anwar nodded his agreement. Was he love-bombing her? Anwar was a collector, she reminded herself. He was a numbers man who prided himself on his many conquests and the elusive artworks he possessed. She told herself that adding a newly discovered artist to his already formidable art collection was his only motive, not believing a word. She wasn't freshly discovered. She was his disgraced lover, fooled by his excessive attention and thrown to the wolves under the weight of false accusations.

Lucy gripped the edge of her catalog as Maria placed red dots beneath the paintings and glided away to add up the sales and tally her commission.

No, Lucy reassured herself. Anwar was acquiring her paintings because they were good. That he would ever be interested in her romantically again was the domain of dreams. Besides, he had betrayed her. She wanted nothing more to do with him. As she turned to leave, Anwar reached out and gently caught her hand. Every whisper of hair on her body rose in heightened awareness as he laced his fingers through hers.

"Don't go."

CHAPTER THREE

"You've made an important acquisition, your Highness. Congratulations," Maria gushed as she pressed glasses bubbling with champagne toward them.

"I'm not drinking," Lucy said, scorchingly aware that Anwar's dark, searching eyes didn't leave her as she politely declined the alcohol and reached for a glass of sparkling water.

"The series reveals Lucy's powerful gifts of expressionism and color," Maria continued. "In Lucy's own words," she said, reading from the catalog, "'*With some paint, I can barely control it; I can only follow its lead. It tells me how it wants to be painted.*'"

Years of advising wealthy and discerning collectors on what to buy for their collections had taught Lucy that artists' statements were a critical component of marketing the arts. Still, she hated the hype, especially when talking about her own work.

She painted simply because it made her happy. It made her forget her trauma. It made her forget about Anwar and the pain he had inflicted. Instead, she painted their love story. The one she had dreamed of, the illusion only painting could make real.

"Don't you just love the glints of gold, the giant expanses of the canvas, flowing with orange-reds and turquoise greens, dancing like prisms of light across the wash of baby blue?" Maria said as her gaze drifted to the vast abstract landscape writhing in a rainbow of luscious curves running the length of the far wall. "The works are so evocative. Layered with subtle memories of things seen and loved. Pregnant with possibility."

Lucy gulped. If Maria could read the unspoken secrets beneath the layers, could he?

"The collection is a *tour de force*, a canvas full of joy," Anwar agreed, turning to Lucy as Maria drifted toward a bunch of European collectors chatting with their peers about commissioning a series of works.

"The painting made you lose control?" Anwar drawled teasingly, thinly disguising the memory of the night he stole her virginity. "How did the works want to be painted?" he said, trailing his finger over the honey-hued dunes rounded like naked breasts. "What stories do they tell?" Anwar asked.

"Tales of independence and autonomy and, above all else, freedom," Lucy said unhesitatingly.

"Freedom?"

She nodded. "From fear."

"What is it that you fear?" Anwar drawled as his powerful frame moved closer to her.

You, she wanted to say as her traitorous body blazed with heat. "All my life, I've been marinated in fear. Fear of abandonment. Fear of loss. I wanted to feel forever love," she exclaimed, wishing she had kept her mouth shut.

He would never know how much she had once loved him,

how she still loved him, how she would always love him. She couldn't be one of those women. A victim. A fool. A prisoner. *Not for love*. He had taken everything she had given him with the fullness of her hopeful heart, and he had callously tossed her aside with no more reverence than a dishrag.

"This love will never fade," she flung at him, sweeping her fingers meters from the thickly applied magenta in the painting. "These colors are commitment keepers," she said, "Three coats of UV protective varnish will ensure that," she quickly added. "Of course, don't place it in direct sunlight."

Just like she wouldn't be shining the light on her pregnancy, Lucy vowed as she slid her palms over the stiff folds of her shapeless, noir-black upside-down dress. The touch of tarpaulin did an adequate job of disguising her tiny bump, but even this wouldn't detract from what she considered her biggest failing—*stuffing up parenthood*.

She'd always dreamed of being a mother and a loving, *loved*, wife. Now, she'd been impregnated by a man who could never give her what her child and she both needed. She'd let herself down. Worse, now she was inflicting her reckless mistake on an innocent child. He would be born out of wedlock and never know his father.

And then there was the matter of Anwar's brutal betrayal.

"Why are you exhibiting now?" Anwar asked, jolting her back to the threat her condition posed.

How could she tell him, 'Because I need the money? Because I'm having your baby. Because I'll be raising him on my own without you.'

Instead, she said, "I wanted to challenge myself. I wanted to see if it could be done. *What I could do*," she corrected. "To sell my art instead of being the one promoting other artists."

"You hid it from me," he challenged.

For a stomach-clenching, heart-stopping moment, Lucy froze. He knows. Anwar knows. She forced a look of carefree innocence and smiled, careful to keep any hint of deception shuttered. How could he possibly know the truth, she cautioned. Her baby bump was so unusually tiny that she barely showed.

"Your talent. It's magnificent," Anwar said, returning his gaze to the painting. "The way you've captured the Kingdom of Avana. It's fantastical, whimsical, playful—yet thought-provoking."

Lucy hoped the whoosh of relief that gusted from her mouth wasn't perceptible.

Anwar's head was slightly bowed, but she could see his eyes were fixed in sadness and longing.

"I couldn't wait to leave Avana for most of my life. My brother Tariq told me that one day I would understand the preciousness of the land." He turned to Lucy, his eyes shining. "You have captured the soul of the kingdom. It is Avana, but it is, as you say, a landscape from your mind. I love it."

She gulped hard and swallowed the urge to tell him the truth—the paintings weren't from her mind. They were landscapes from her heart.

"Abstract painting may look simple," she said, referencing the broad planes of color rendered in sensuous sweeps, "but it takes me hours to get the proportions and colors just right."

She continued with what she hoped was a dispassionate, rational analysis of the works, wanting to wipe her heart free of the great compliment he had bestowed upon her. If Anwar truly understood why her paintings held the soul of Avana, the consequences would be disastrous. She needed to distance herself from him and the desert kingdom where their son was conceived.

Lucy pressed the catalog in her hand to her belly and held it there, feeling the warmth and the longing for the child she never thought she'd conceive.

She had trusted Anwar with her future once. And he had abandoned her. She needed to leave. Her eyes darted toward the entrance.

"Are you going to do another runner?" Anwar said, registering her panicked glance toward the door. His smoldering gaze narrowed and flowed to her palm, still pressed against her stomach.

Heat flared in her belly. "Runner? We both know why I had to leave Avana," she hissed under her breath. "You've conveniently forgotten your role in detonating the art advisory firm I spent my life building."

"About that—" Anwar began.

"So that's why you're really here." Her gaze darted around the gallery, anxiously registering if anyone had overheard her careless revelation of the past she fought to keep hidden.

"I want to resolve this as discreetly as possible."

CHAPTER FOUR

Lucy watched with mixed feelings as the art enthusiasts, fully sated after immersing themselves in her creativity, prepared to leave her art exhibition. She didn't want to be left alone with Anwar, but what choice did she have, she mused as they swelled around the entrance.

Suddenly, a collective gasp rippled through the groups of people, drawing Lucy and Anwar's attention to the street. The hum of anticipation grew louder as a sleek, gleaming gold Lamborghini, adorned with intricate designs and polished to perfection, effortlessly glided to a graceful halt in front of the gallery.

The crowd parted, their gazes fixated on the opulence before them. Whoever was behind the wheel relished the attention, Lucy reflected.

The Lamborghini seemed to radiate its own gravitational force, capturing the attention of everyone within its vicinity. The car's gilded exterior reflected New York's cityscape and caught the last rays of the sun, dazzling onlookers with its fiery brilliance.

Lucy dragged her gaze away and stole a glance at Anwar, appreciating his understated, quiet elegance for the first time. Anwar may be many things, but he was not a show-off, she thought as she turned to see the sleek gull-wing doors lifting upwards.

"It's Prince Sheikh Fazza na Hassir," she overheard someone say. Lucy had never met Anwar's younger brother, but his arrival in New York had been well-publicized. The jet-setting sheikh was renowned for traveling with his fleet of cars to different cities, collecting various lingerie models to keep him sated. Every tabloid and gossip column had covered his recent arrival, but no one at Lucy's opening had expected to see the Playboy prince in person. Least of all Lucy. Hell, she hadn't even expected to see Anwar.

Fazza's tailored suit, meticulously fitted, accentuated his commanding presence as he stepped out, exuding an air of confidence and playful refinement. His blue, penetrating eyes surveyed the surroundings, capturing the curiosity of those who had gathered.

Whispers of admiration and awe swept through the crowd, a symphony of hushed voices marveling at the convergence of exquisite machinery and remarkable wealth. All eyes were drawn to this unexpected arrival. As the young sheikh approached the entrance, palpable energy coursed through the crowd. Cameras clicked, and flashes illuminated the air, capturing this magical moment, eager to immortalize the intersection of opulence and artistic expression. The allure of this golden apparition, juxtaposed against the backdrop of New York's creative hub, created a visual spectacle that was impossible to ignore.

"The publicity will be amazing," Maria said, drawing to Lucy's side. "Priceless."

Lucy wasn't so sure. But what was priceless was Fazza's

timing. Hopefully, Anwar's brother's arrival would divert his attention long enough for her to quietly and quickly make a discreet and rapid exit.

Her heart pulsed as she watched with a mix of apprehension and curiosity as the sheikh seamlessly transitioned from the realm of luxury cars to the domain of artistic exploration, pausing to admire *Desert Dreams* at the entrance.

As the exhibition doors beckoned him inside, the crowd followed suit. Eager to discover what had captured his attention and who he was here to meet. The echoes of excitement reverberated through the gallery walls, blending with the city's vibrant energy.

"Anwar," Fazza said, throwing his arms around his bemused brother. "I hope I am on time."

"Subtle as always—and late, but this time it was fated," Anwar said, gazing momentarily toward Lucy.

But it wasn't Lucy that captured Fazza's attention. "Who is that gorgeous creature?" he stammered, nodding toward the woman at the center of the room, her long, ebony hair cascading down her back like a silk waterfall.

"Grace Hunt," Anwar replied. "I doubt your showoff Lamborghini will impress her."

"Women love it."

"Not this one."

"What makes you so sure?" Fazza said petulantly.

"She's with the competition."

"How so?"

"Grace Hunt is the newly appointed Chairwoman of Ferrari."

Anwar watched as his younger brother, unable to resist her magnetic pull, found himself drawn towards Grace. He approached her with the confidence of a man accustomed to getting what he desired, but this time, his desire ran deeper than mere attraction, and Anwar knew it. He should. Hadn't the same reckless interest nearly cost him his kingdom?

"Let's go, Fazza," Anwar commanded, tugging his brother by the sleeve. "We're already late." He beckoned to Maria Bright. "I have an urgent matter to attend to but have not finished my business here. Please arrange a private viewing in the gallery of the collection I purchased tonight."

Maria arched her eyebrows.

"Please ensure the artist is present and no one else."

"I think Lucy has plans tonight."

"Tell her to change them," Anwar commanded in a tone that made it clear that failing to fulfill his quest would have serious financial repercussions.

"Of course, Your Highness."

As Anwar climbed into the Lamborghini, he turned to look once more at the woman who had evaded him for so long. He smiled as he saw Maria approach Lucy to tell her he had summoned her for a private viewing. Lucy took a step back, shaking her head. He saw her mouth form the words, "Why?" and then begin to protest. He smirked with satisfaction. He didn't need to see anymore. Lucy's resistance was futile. He had found her, and there would be no escape this time.

CHAPTER FIVE

A rt enthralled him. Locating rare pieces, acquiring the unattainable, and shuffling priceless paintings between the palatial homes and palaces dotted around the world always satisfied him. Art spoke to his soul and healed the wounds of parental neglect. Art soothed him. It was one of the reasons Anwar had bucked family tradition and chosen his particular line of work. If you could call indulging his passion work, that was.

He was rebellious enough to choose any profession that defied family tradition, but becoming one of the world's most famous art collectors had the added benefit of allowing him to surround himself with things he loved. Not people who were far too flawed and fickle, but paintings that improved with age—in value and beauty.

He had very definite opinions on what he liked and didn't like. He was discerning, unlike his Russian counterparts, who purchased art purely to elevate their status. He did not need that. He was the son of a king, born into royalty, and a natural leader. When he chose paintings, especially by new and upcoming artists, their fortunes were favorably fated.

He liked that he could elevate others, not to feed his ego but because of the joy their paintings created. When he found a painting that spoke to his soul, he would inevitably acquire it, whatever the cost. This was the reason, the only reason he had purchased all the artworks in Lucy's exhibition.

How could a woman with eyes like hers have done anything criminal? Whatever the answers were, he was dead set on one thing— ensuring harmony within his family. His brother Hamad had been insistent that Lucy had defrauded him, setting him up to spend a fortune on a painting now everyone believed worthless.

Though it might be considered one of those escapist fantasies Anwar was sometimes accused of possessing, he wanted to believe she was innocent of any wrongdoing. Hamad, less so. Ultimately, there was no choice but to sever Lucy's curatorial services and expel her from the kingdom, for her sake as much as anything. His brother's vengeful nature was well known. Once crossed, Hamad never forgave. Perhaps it was the scorpion in him.

The evidence Hamad presented to Anwar and his other brothers supporting his fraud claim was compelling. Copies of correspondence, email exchanges, and Lucy's recommen-dation of the art expert tasked with authenticating the painting left little doubt of her crime. It was better for everyone, espe-cially Lucy, that he had consciously aided and abetted her escape. Had he deliberately led her to believe he was expelling her? Had he severed her contract to save her the indignity of being brought to trial under Arabic law? All these thoughts weighed on him now.

CHAPTER SIX

Anwar had said he wanted to settle matters discretely. Did that mean dangerously, Lucy wondered, as she unlocked the door to the art gallery that evening?

Why did Anwar want a private viewing? He had made his purchase. The deal was done. That left what? The lure of a personal conquest? To take the only thing Lucy had left to give? Was that what he meant when he reappeared in her life and told her he wanted to resolve their past discretely? Well, he would be disappointed. Lucy would never yield to any arrogant, self-entitled claim he felt he had over her.

Concern wormed through her gut as she surveyed the dimly lit space filled with mystery and enchantment. Maria had left the lights on low, ensuring Lucy's paintings were exquisitely spotlighted. "We don't want the Sheikh suffering buyer's remorse and changing his mind," Maria had said, handing Lucy the keys and reminding her to turn off the lights when she left. "We want to ensure Anwar remains enchanted—then maybe he'll return for more."

More! Lucy didn't want Anwar coming back for more.

The less she saw of him, the better. But she hadn't been able to tell Maria that. If only she could have confided in her and saved them both from the over-the-top ordeal. Instead, Maria had channeled her inner movie star director and curated the encounter like a love scene in a romantic play.

Soft classical music filled the air, its melodious notes floating gently from hidden speakers, providing a romantic soundtrack to the evening. The music, combined with the soothing ambiance of the gallery, was expertly curated to create an atmosphere that encouraged heartfelt conversation and stolen glances. The seductive scent of oil paint and varnish mingled with the lingering aroma of exotic perfumes worn by beautiful women at her opening. To the left, near Maria's gleaming white marble desk, a giant crystal vase bloomed with scented orchids and magnolias expertly created by celebrity florist Rose Lilly.

The whole room looked magical, like a harem to love, Lucy muttered under her breath as Anwar strode into the art gallery, looking like he owned the place. *Owned her*, Lucy conceded to her dismay.

His dark gaze fastened on her with such searing intensity it made her skin burn with self-awareness. All she wanted to do was run away, but she had no choice but to do his bidding.

"You've gone to a lot of trouble," he purred.

Danger prickled down her spine, fracturing the reserve she had so carefully erected. "I didn't," she shot back, thrusting her arms over her chest.

What little protest she had initially offered when Maria had told her of Anwar's demand for a private viewing had been quickly extinguished. They both needed the injection of cash that Anwar's purchase of Lucy's collection had provided. Without Maria, there would have been no solo exhibition. She owed it to her. But to Anwar, she owed nothing, Lucy reminded herself. But here they were. Together. Alone. Nothing to keep them apart but memories she refused to rekindle.

"Why did you keep your talent a secret from me?" The steely glint in Anwar's eyes warned that he would not be diverted from his purpose.

"It was a private passion," Lucy threw at him. "At least it was until I suddenly found myself out of a job."

"You blame *me*?"

"I had always painted as a hobby," she continued, refusing to dignify his arrogant denial with her rebuttal.

His gaze trawled the length of her body, then rose to her face and lingered on her lips. "You have a God-given gift, Lucy."

Lucy wiped her mouth and shrugged. She couldn't allow herself to fall prey to his kindness. Not again. She pressed her hand to her belly, feeling the emptiness and longing. She was doing the right thing. It was better for everyone that their child remained a secret. *Wasn't it?*

Doubt and fear crawled through the lining of her gut as his dark brows knitted together in puzzled surprise. He was staring at her belly, she thought with alarm. Why? Did he know? No, that was impossible. She barely showed.

She racked her mind, scrambling for ways to divert Anwar's attention from the uncomfortable truth.

"Some years ago, my mother looked up at a painting of a woman on the wall of her dining room, and she asked me, 'Why can't I have a painting of my mother? I thought I'd create a portrait of my grandmother as a surprise gift so my mother could hang it on her wall. I took classes, studied books on portrait painting, and tried to master the skill. To please my mother. I was always trying to please her, never realizing it was futile. I would never win my mother's affection. She never wanted me," Lucy said, instantly regretting her disclosure.

She froze as Anwar feasted his dark gaze on her. She wanted to flee from his penetrating stare and the magnetic attraction that wrapped an electric force field around them, stained with the tainted memories that united them both.

"In my culture, we believe we choose our parents." Anwar smiled dangerously as his eyes traveled over her breasts.

She crossed her arms over her chest protectively, conscious that her pregnancy had made them more prominent. She hoped he had forgotten how they felt that night they had made love—or even, if he hadn't, that he'd be too distracted now to care. A whoosh of relief escaped her mouth as he turned his attention toward her paintings.

"We believe that before birth, our souls are bestowed with talents because of this choice," he said.

"My mother had nothing to do with my creativity." Lucy snapped. "My grandmother taught me to paint."

His formidable gaze searched her face, then drifted to her thumping heart. "Perhaps your grandmother guided your conception when you were born," he conceded.

Lucy suddenly felt grateful to Anwar for rekindling her nostalgic feelings. Her grandmother had been more nurturing and kinder to her than her mother ever had.

"Yes, I think quite possibly she was," she said, her voice dropping to a whisper. "I felt connected to my grandmother as I painted her portrait. I would sing and talk to her, even though she had died many years earlier."

Just like she had sung and talked to their unborn child as she created the works in her exhibition, Lucy reflected as she felt a little kick in her belly. Anwar could never know that. He could never know of the child conceived in one ill-fated night of passion. His way of life, his Kingdom's views on social issues, their customs, were all too different. Anwar's world was alien to everything she wanted for her life.

She was suddenly aware of the irregular bump of her heart as the blazing heat of his presence engulfed her. Anwar's sex hormones were steroids for fertility. *And fantasy.* How long could she stand beside her son's father and pretend she didn't care? How long could she keep her dangerous secret?

Her traitorous body might still dream of Anwar, but she could never surrender, she affirmed inwardly. Not if she wanted to retain her freedom.

"It's a bitter-sweet tale," Lucy continued, reluctantly focusing on the story of her childhood trauma instead of the pain he had inflicted. "When I told my mother that my portrait of my grandmother was a finalist in a prestigious portraiture competition, she said nothing."

"That's appalling! What sort of mother wouldn't encourage their child? She should have been proud."

His voice swept over her skin as if he'd kissed her. Panicked at the attraction his sympathy instilled in her, she whirled around to face him, forcing a frosty dignity she was far from feeling. "A lot of children suffer worse hurts from their parents."

His dark gaze probed the fearful confusion in her eyes.

"Everyone told me what a great accolade it was to be selected," Lucy blurted. "I told my mother that as a finalist, they would like to hang the painting for two weeks in an exhibition. Instead of being pleased for me, she refused to let me take the painting for the short-term show. 'It's mine,' she said, refusing to let me borrow it from her so I could exhibit it."

"Why did she behave so awfully?"

"Maybe her mother never said kind words to her." She was revealing too much. Saying too much. Inviting too much. Still, perhaps if he knew how screwed up her family was—*she was*—he might leave her alone.

"My grandmother was a beautiful, gifted piano player, singer, and painter. But she battled alcohol addiction all her life. When she had a few drinks, she said the most horrible things."

"Family!" Anwar said sympathetically.

"I knew it was the drink talking," Lucy offered in defense of her grandmother. "She had suffered so much trauma. I don't blame her. Her father got into a drunken brawl and killed a man. She was sent into foster care when she was four and never saw her brother or parents again."

Anwar's eyes locked on Lucy. "You never mentioned this at your job interview."

"You were hiring me, not my family," she said forcefully.

"If it weren't for me, you wouldn't have started painting again, would you?" Anwar said with righteous arrogance.

Lucy scowled. "It always has to be about you, doesn't it?"

He smiled dangerously as he looked down at the forbidden place where their bodies had once pressed together. She felt a hot pulse of need and fear sweep over her and settle like a lightning bolt between her legs.

He advanced toward her. She bucked against him as his powerful arms pressed her against the wall. He laughed. "Not just me. Us." He bent down and pressed his mouth upon hers, silencing her protests.

There was nothing then but the fire of desire that fanned through her, one bright flame after another, torching all resistance.

Anwar pressed the proof of his need hard against her. His mouth bent to her breasts, teasing them through her dress, while his hands streaked beneath her hem, testing her shape, rising between her legs to her belly.

"Stop!" she cried out, hoping he had not discovered her secret. He dropped his hand and stepped back while she smoothed her crumpled dress.

Anwar stood above her, his dark face stern and his golden eyes glittering. "I believe congratulations are in order," he said in a low, rough voice.

"Congratulations?" she stammered. "What do you mean?"

"You succeeded in distracting me. How long do you think you will evade me?"

* * *

Permanently, Lucy thought the next day as she prepared to shower. Whatever matter Anwar had wanted to settle discretely remained a hot topic. At least as far as Anwar was concerned. Maria had already transferred an advance on the commissions earned from selling her paintings. She would leave Manhattan and enjoy a much-needed break before the birth of her son. Hopefully, Anwar would lose interest in pursuing the matter and be long gone by the time she returned.

She didn't want to think about the thick, dark fall of hair that brushed her face as he kissed her. She didn't want to think about how her treacherous body burned with need in his presence. She didn't want to think about why he had reappeared in her life.

No matter how much she craved affection, she couldn't afford to think about Anwar at all. The sooner she was out of his reach, the happier and safer she and her unborn child would be.

CHAPTER SEVEN

W hen Anwar arrived at Lucy's apartment, he was shocked to find the door ajar. Did she have no concern for her safety? Her carelessness troubled as much as it infuriated him. She needed protecting, he thought to his chagrin. Not because he cared about her, he told himself, noticing the lurch in his gut calling him a liar. He cared only for himself and the continuity of his legacy. He had the element of surprise. She thought he hadn't detected her secret, he affirmed as he stepped into Lucy's small, unassuming apartment.

The vibrant atmosphere that met him was as surprising as it was astonishing. Despite its modest size and Lucy's limited resources, her humble dwelling burst with creativity and inspiration.

The living area was modestly furnished, yet the space pulsed with her unique energy. An impressive collection of paintings, sketches, and photographs adorned the walls, each capturing the essence of the landscape he recognized immediately as Avana. While the collection of her paintings he had purchased were landscapes from her mind, these passionate renderings were clearly from her soul, he mused as he noticed his heart pulse. Could the woman who had deceived him have found a route into the fortress he strove so hard to erect?

No, he vowed silently. They were paintings, inanimate artworks. That was all he told himself as a subtle spell wove around him. He folded his arms over his chest. No matter what magic Lucy may feel the artworks possessed, no matter the temptation or pleasures she promised, he knew he couldn't succumb. He had come to New York seeking redemption for this family, and now he had discovered her secret pregnancy.

She thought he hadn't registered the tiny swell of her belly last night, but it had not gone unnoticed. But he would not confess that he knew until he could ensure she would not escape again. Once she had served her purpose, he would leave Lucy alone. Once and for all.

Where was she, he wondered as he strolled through the living space. The kitchenette was tiny yet efficiently organized, and the shelves overflowed with vibrant mismatched plates and mugs, reflecting Lucy's eclectic taste. The air was infused with the smell of freshly brewed coffee mingling with the remnants of paint and the faint hum of creative energy.

His eyes were drawn to the half-finished canvases lining a narrow hallway leading to what looked like her bedroom. The door was slightly ajar. Another security breach! Did the infuriating woman think she was untouchable? He would soon relieve her of that naive belief, he thought as he entered the cozy sanctuary she had created, adorned with an iconic lava lamp that cast a bright rouge glow upon the room.

The bed was adorned with a patchwork quilt, creating a haven of comfort and tranquillity. Despite the lack of wealth and luxury Anwar was used to, there was something, dare he admit it, heartwarming about her sweet abode. He grimaced. To indulge in such sentimentalities would be fatal.

A small studio space was tucked away in the corner of Lucy's bedroom. Canvases of all sizes adorned the walls, displaying her vivid imagination and skill and reflecting the ever-evolving nature of her mind. Easels stood proudly, holding works in progress, and a cluttered desk was home to an array of paints, brushes, and other supplies.

Anwar was astonished and inspired by Lucy's resourcefulness. Somehow, she had transformed her simple apartment into a vibrant haven of artistic expression. Despite the limited resources available to her, she had managed to pursue her passion and create a beautiful oasis amid the bustling, chaotic metropolis of New York City.

He wondered how her creativity would flourish if she could inhabit a space a thousand times more significant. That was not his concern, he affirmed as a muffled sound of running water reached his ears. A symphony of droplets cascading onto tiles heightened his senses. Desire and intrigue urged him forward. He gently pushed the door to the bathroom open. Steam billowed out, obscuring his view momentarily before dissipating to unveil Lucy, enveloped in a cloud of ethereal mist.

His heart slammed against his chest as she stepped from the shower, her silhouette illuminated by softly glowing sunlight filtering through the frosted window. Droplets of water adorned her radiant porcelain skin like delicate pearls. He held his breath lest her awareness break the trance of feminine grace. Her slender fingers, adorned with large paint-splattered rings, ran through her dampened locks, coaxing rivulets of water to trickle down her shoulders.

A sense of reverence washed over Anwar as he observed this intimate moment, realizing that he had unintentionally invaded her private sanctuary. In that instant, he understood the profound beauty of this encounter, transcending the boundaries of wealth and status. Two souls, worlds apart, yet bound by the shared appreciation for life's simple pleasures, he mused.

The sheikh and the artist. They were momentarily suspended in time, transcending their differences, connected through the vulnerability and innocence of a beautiful woman stepping out of a shower. In that fleeting moment, he knew that even he, a billionaire sheikh with everything money could possess, could find solace and inspiration amidst ordinary moments. True wealth, he affirmed, lay not in material opulence but in the beauty discovered in unexpected places.

His body pulsed with an animalistic desire to claim Lucy and make love to her in the shower. His poise faltered as he tried to regain control. He wanted to engulf her in his embrace, hold her tight against him, and possess her sweet mouth in his hungry lips. It took every ounce of his self-restraint to hold back the torrent of sharp, almost manic delirium that threatened to drown him.

He forced his gaze to her. How he would love to scoop her wet, sensuous body into his arms, look into her startled eyes as he strode across to the soft quilt, and lay her down on her back. How he would love to claim the pleasure he knew awaited, driving them both to heights of stolen passion.

Instead, he bent his formidable will back to his sole purpose. Silently, he retreated from the scene, leaving her to reclaim her privacy. He retraced his footsteps, returned to the apartment door, and knocked loudly. As his fist rapped on the darkened timber of the door, he fortified his resolve. This was not a time to indulge in nostalgic dreams of lust and intimacy. Lucy had kept the truth from him. Now, she must pay the price of her deception.

CHAPTER EIGHT

"Anwar! What are you doing here?" Lucy's heart pounded as she registered Anwar's smoldering eyes surveying the floor-length fuchsia kaftan clinging to her damp skin.

"I thought we could go sightseeing."

"I can't. I'll be late." She had nowhere to go, nowhere to be—other than to flee. But she wouldn't tell Anwar that.

"Late for what?" Anwar pressed.

"Stuff," she said, coiling rivulets of wet hair around her fingers and wringing excess moisture from the damp locks.

God, he was arrogant, she thought as droplets of water pooled on her bare feet. Did he think he had a monopoly on living an interesting, unrestricted life? Of course, he did. Being an infinitely eligible prince, the son of a king. Not a struggling artist and soon-to-be solo mother. Anwar could indulge all his sensual pleasures without fear or restraint—forever and always.

If it weren't for the knowledge that, thanks to his purchase of all her paintings, she could pay her rent arrears and escape for a short-term break, she would push him out the door and tell him to disappear. Her dire finances worried her. How could they not? She didn't have just herself to worry about now, but providing for her child.

Their child.

It would be much easier to surrender her freedom and tell Anwar the truth. But she would never yield to his wealth for fear of being controlled, a prisoner to his precarious pleasure.

She would find a way to make her own fortune and provide for her son. Last night, Anwar, without realizing it, had already helped her make a good start. A perfect start. She was no longer a starving artist. For the next six months, anyway. Her commission earned from the exhibition assured that. And then, who knew what the future held?

"I want to show you something," Anwar said.

"What?"

"I don't want to tell you something. I want to *show* you something," he commanded.

Lucy straightened and stared at him.

"How did you find out where I lived?"

"Are you coming?"

"No. I have stuff to do." She could not possibly go anywhere with him even if she wanted to.

"Let me drive you," he said, his gaze lingering over the thin cotton that clung to Lucy's erect nipples.

"You?"

"My chauffeur," he corrected.

Resistance, she knew, would be futile. What Anwar wanted, Anwar always got. *Always.*

"I need to finish getting dressed. I've just got out of the shower."

"I know," he said.

Why was he smirking? She wondered as she padded back to the bathroom and ran the dryer through her hair.

She tried to shrug off the feelings of foreboding as she finished getting dressed and thrust her feet into a pair of sparkly open-toe sandals.

"You didn't say where we were going," she remarked questioningly as they walked along the corridor and down the three flights of stairs to street level.

His mouth quirked teasingly. "Somewhere uniquely special. I think you owe me one surprise."

"Do I?" she said as they climbed into Anwar's waiting limousine. "Why the mystery?"

His gaze drifted past her and fell upon the graffiti covering her apartment's exterior walls. The once pristine facade now bore a creation by the infamous artist Jean-Michel Basquiat. The artist's signature chaotic style mirrored the turmoil that flooded her body as Anwar's eyes darkened.

His lips formed a contemptuous line as he turned to her. "What is that desecration?"

"Art," Lucy replied.

"Not in my culture," he said. "Such horrors are symbolic of disrespect and disregard."

Yes, she thought. How could he possibly understand the passion and purpose street artists poured into their works? Basquiat was the epitome of everything the Anwar detested. With his rebellious nature and disregard for societal norms, the artist was celebrated in the art world for his unique vision. But to Anwar, Basquiat's drug-fueled, child-like scrawls were nothing more than the mark-making of a common criminal intent on defiling property with his defiance.

Was that what Anwar would think of her when he discovered the truth of her resistance to do what was expected of her? She wondered with concern as she saw the Sheikh's infuriated expression.

With a clenched fist, Anwar summoned his driver to begin their journey. "Let's get out of this wretched place."

"Why won't you tell me where we are going?" Lucy said as they crawled through the gridlocked Manhattan streets.

"I told you. I'm showing you something."

"Something where?" she asked as they crossed the Hudson River.

They rode in strained silence until the limousine entered an airfield and stopped in front of Anwar's private jet. She recognized the black and gold family crest emblazoned on the outside, featuring a sleek and powerful falcon with razor-sharp talons piercing its prey. Lucy gripped the door arm and momentarily considered screaming as Anwar opened the car door and gestured for her to exit.

Keep calm, she told herself. Keep calm and act like everything is working out for your highest good, she repeated, referencing the affirmations she had memorized since being banished from Anwar's kingdom.

She reluctantly exited the limo, feigning supreme nonchalance as Anwar pressed the small of her back and guided her up the stairs to the aircraft's luxurious cabin.

This can't be happening.

"The other night in the gallery—the way the light caught the silk of your dress, your silhouette, the way my hand felt —" he said.

Oh, no. He knows.

"Are you pregnant, *habibti*?"

Lucy, whose parents had lied about everything, suddenly found herself trapped. She nodded, forcing her lips together, fighting a response to the question she knew would surely follow.

"Is the child mine?" His hand lingered over the aircraft door, the gateway to her freedom.

How could she lie? Hiding, running, and fleeing was one thing, but lying was quite another. Hadn't she vowed she would never be like her parents?

She entered the cabin and collapsed into the leather-padded seat. Leaning into the softness, she anticipated Anwar's rage barrelling upon her when he discovered the truth of her deception.

She saw his gaze ease down the width of her belly. She shifted awkwardly, breaking the tension between them, and glanced around the cabin. She was surrounded by luxury. Muted desert tones, aesthetically pleasing curvaceous leather couches, and elegant marble tables gilded with gold caught the last rays of the sun. Anwar's jet oozed luxury and style, yet she felt like she was in a gilded jail. One stolen glance at Anwar told Lucy her captor was determined to throw away the key.

"Yes," she whispered. Her gaze drifted to the carefully crafted interior doors reminiscent of angel wings. All she wanted was her freedom. Now, her mere admission sealed her fate. "The child is yours," she said, facing him.

His expression froze. He regarded her as a vessel, an inanimate object to possess for this ruthless purpose.

"When is the child due?"

"In twelve weeks."

"And the sex?"

"What about the sex?" Lucy said.

"Do you know? Boy or girl?"

"We are having a boy," she said, revealing her scan results.

"I could not be happier," his voice held no emotion as he turned and glanced out the windows.

"*You're happy?*" she said incredulously.

41

He turned and regarded her intently, a vague concern in his gaze.

"Feelings have nothing to do with it. The fact is, my circumstances have changed."

His circumstances were none of her business. Lucy was resolute in that. Her eyes darted to the cabin door, desperate to escape, but she knew it was too late. She saw Anwar's brows furrow.

"I need an heir," he said fiercely. "A legitimate heir, not a bastard child. And for that, I will need a wife."

CHAPTER NINE

Lucy stared at him as if she couldn't believe what he'd said. The fact was he was left with no choice.

"Why, out of all the women at your whim and call, would you want me, the runaway, as your very inconvenient and fraudulent wife?" she said tersely. "I'm sure you have plenty of lovers queuing for the opportunity to legitimize your legacy."

He frowned. "These are precarious times. Neighboring warlords have their eyes on Avana. They covet what we have. The happiness. The wealth. The freedom. They seek to destroy. They distort the Arabic faith in their grab for power. Imposing Sharia Law on their people, silencing, shrouding, and shaming their women. Denying them education and the equality my brothers and I have vowed to ensure for our people."

He stared at her, his face tight with grim purpose. "We must stand our ground and fortify our commitment to democracy."

"I don't see what this has to do with me." She pressed her body into the seat and turned her legs away. "I've spent my life marinating in danger," she mumbled as she stared out the window. "Never knowing when I was going to be emotionally and psychologically attacked." She spun around to face him. "And now you're bringing me, *us*, to a warzone?"

"You're being overly dramatic. Things have not escalated to that level. I am being preventative. Fortifying Avana's future."

"But they could invade, couldn't they?"

"The forces of evil will never win. But it is not through want of trying," he conceded. "They agitate and sow discord amongst our men, creating aggression in men of peace. They are the cause of the wave of Islamophobia spreading through democracies around the Western world. They shame us all with this stain. People fear Islam and Muslims because these psychopathic, extremist tyrants have corrupted what is beautiful with their ugliness. They deny the truth and speak in lies."

She exhaled noisily. "This is exactly why I hadn't wanted to return to Avana. *Ever*. It's surrounded by a hotbed of hostility."

"The world is a volcano of hostility, *habibti.*"

"Yes," she agreed. "It seems like everyone is in love with war."

"Peace is my passion," Anwar said. "I will do what I must to protect it." *Even marrying the woman who betrayed my trust.*

Lucy's fear simmered through the aircraft cabin. Her vulnerability stirred his passion. Anwar wanted to ensure her fears were never realized, to protect her at all costs.

"They will not win," he said to reassure her. "With a wife, I hold more power. Especially in the eyes of my people."

"How romantic," Lucy said, her tone marinated in sarcasm. "Besides, I thought you swore you'd never marry."

"You are carrying my heir. The only possible way we will maintain our sovereignty is to fortify our family line. To leave the responsibility for the continuity of our lineage to my brother, Tariq, would be reckless," he pressed his lips into a fierce line. "If something happened to him—"

"But what if something happened to you?"

The worry etched in her voice caused his gut to churn. Nobody had ever worried about what happened to him. He wanted to tell her that. But he decided the best option was to bend his formidable will to his purpose.

"If something should happen to me, my lineage must continue. I have deferred long enough. I do not want to be an old father as mine was. Time is of the essence, and you, *habibti*, pregnant as you are, will achieve that deliverable goal quickly."

CHAPTER TEN

The sun slowly dipped below the horizon, casting a flaming array of colors across the sky as Anwar's private jet soared beyond Manhattan. The irony was not lost on Lucy. Many women would kill to be in her position. Anwar had reassured her that she was in no imminent danger, in many ways, quite the opposite.

She was being spirited away from a life of struggle onboard a luxurious private jet belonging to the enigmatic billionaire Sheikh Anwar na Hassir, pregnant with his child, and an offer of marriage. If you could call a demand a marriage proposal, that was.

Despite her fury, she couldn't help but admire Anwar. He didn't run away from danger. He faced it. He prepared for it. He conquered tyrants, despots, and fools. Despite her fury at being taken from her home, she found herself respecting Anwar's conviction that aggressors would never win. If only she had someone fighting for her in that way.

The jet soared through the clouds, ascending higher into the atmosphere, as Lucy's thoughts drifted to Anwar. He was a powerful man with an insatiable passion for peace and art.

Those things alone should make him attractive. As she settled into her plush seat, she couldn't help but feel apprehensive.

Their passion for art had united them from the start. But now, her breakout exhibition, *Desert Dreams*, had taken an unexpected turn, forever altering the course of her life. He had once sought her expertise in curating his private collection, and now *she* was to be part of his collection. Her self-reliance was her rock, and now he was crushing it.

She should never have agreed to get into that damned limousine.

Suddenly, the sound of fluttering wings drew her attention to the rear of the jet. Lucy turned to see a magnificent falcon perched near the far window. Its piercing gaze locked onto Lucy as if assessing her worthiness to be in its master's life. Fascinated by the bird's powerful beauty, Lucy couldn't help but feel a strange connection. If only she could be that fierce, she thought.

And that loved.

Anwar's devotion to his falcon was well-known, matched only by the obsession his older brother Tariq shared to rehabilitate injured birds and protect other animals from harm in the sanctuary he had created in the kingdom of Avana. Would she find sanctuary in Anwar's extended family? Lucy wondered anxiously as the jet continued its seven-hour journey.

She glanced up as Anwar emerged from his private chamber, dressed impeccably in a long white *dishdashi* that emphasized the elegance of his powerful physique.

Anwar approached her with a wry smile, his eyes sparkling with the satisfaction of his conquest. He gestured towards the falcon perched by the window. "I see you have met Zephyr," he said in a deep, melodic voice. "He is my most loyal companion. Like you, Lucy, he possesses a unique ability to sense beauty. *And authenticity.* I believe his presence will enhance our life together."

"I don't think he likes me," she said, her voice barely above a whisper.

"Trust is earned," Anwar said, running his fingers down Zephyr's dark brown back feathers. "You must prove you are worthy of devotion."

Tension needled her arms. That was just the point. She wasn't worthy, was she? If she had been, Anwar would never have thrown her out of his Kingdom in the first place. And now, he had suddenly decided she was worthy of being his wife. And yet he couldn't stand to be in her company, she thought as he disappeared with his treasured falcon into his private cabin.

Now that Anwar was gone, she felt strangely empty. Could it be that despite the fact he had played her like just another casual encounter, she wanted his love more than she dared admit?

Don't you dare, she vowed inwardly. *Don't you dare be so weak.* Remember what's at stake, she told herself firmly. Find a way to escape.

Lucy woke from a restless sleep just as the jet descended. Manhattan's concrete streets and harsh neon lights were replaced with a breathtaking oasis. Palm trees and exotic flowers swayed gently in the warm breeze. They had returned to a hidden paradise, untouched by the rest of the world.

They were met on the tarmac by a white limousine, which took them on the three-hour drive to Anwar's palace. As they drove past palm trees thick with succulent dates that lined the road, horror crashed through her chest. She was now a foreigner in a land beyond Western law's protection.

She never should have come. But what choice did Anwar give her?

"Will Hamad be here?" Lucy said to Anwar, glancing at the frowning sentries as they approached the entrance to the sprawling palatial estate overlooking the Arabian Sea.

"Recent events have curtailed Hamad's travel," Anwar said, subtly referencing the as-yet unsolved murder of a Western journalist still fresh on everyone's minds.

Lucy shuddered. Many believed Hamad had ordered the hit upon the man critical of his grab for power. But no one could prove it.

"I have not seen my brother for some time. He has been hiding in his palace as though if he is out of sight, he will also be out of mind, and everyone will forget the crime."

A whoosh of air escaped Lucy's lips.

"I will not lie to you. In his eyes, you are a sworn enemy."

"And in yours?"

Anwar shrugged. "There are things we have still not discussed."

"Is that why you kidnapped me?"

"I have not kidnapped you. Consider yourself detained as my quest until the child is born."

"Am I to be tried again for the crimes your cousin says I committed? The courts in the US and Britain ruled in my favor."

"Colonial empiricists have no jurisdiction here," he said fiercely.

"So you don't believe me."

"I didn't say that."

"But that's why you brought me back."

"Not just that," he said, his gaze drifting to her belly. "I am duty-bound."

"Duty," she spat. "Duty to force me to marry you. Duty to produce your heir. Duty to try me for a crime I did not commit. And then what? Lock me away as your father did to the princesses."

"My father—" Anwar began. He pressed his lips firmly together. "Please, enjoy your return. Enjoy this moment. While you can."

Anwar led Lucy through the opulent halls of his private estate, adorned with priceless works of art from every corner of the globe. Each room showcased a different era and genre. Despite her fear of the future, Lucy felt her heart swell with pride, knowing she had helped curate his collection. Every piece had been meticulously chosen to create an immersive experience. They were beautiful then and were beautiful now. *More beautiful*, she thought, enraptured by the enduring legacy she had helped create.

Zephyr, the falcon, followed them, perched on Anwar's gloved hand, his eyes scanning the surroundings with an unwavering focus. It was as if the bird possessed an innate ability to discern the true essence of the art, its wisdom transcending the limitations of human perception.

Anwar suddenly stopped. "There are no rules here, Lucy. You know that, don't you? There have never been any restrictions between us. I don't want to take your freedom."

"Then I'm free to leave as I please," she said, knowing as she spoke that was the one concession he would never allow until their son was born.

Lucy felt her heart race as he leaned forward, his cheek almost brushing hers. She could see the firm set of his mouth, the searing scrutiny of his gaze, the determined set to his jaw.

"You may do as you like while you are here. But you may not leave."

CHAPTER ELEVEN

"**A**re you serious?" Lucy thrust her hands on her hips. "That's barbaric! I demand you release me. Immediately!"

"That's not possible," Anwar affirmed quietly. His hand crept up to her neck and cupped gently under her chin, lifting her face toward his.

She swallowed hard and forced his hand away. "You are not playing fair!"

"Life is not fair, *habibti*. Don't fall into the entitlement trap of feeling like you're a victim. You're not."

"I'm nobody's victim," she threw at him. "I will not be your kept bride. Do you think kidnapping me will keep me here? You're mistaken! Do you think hijacking my art career will be my ruin? You're mistaken. Do you think forcing me to marry you will make me love you? You're mistaken! I warn you, Anwar. You have bitten off more than your perfect white teeth can chew!"

Anwar smiled with the arrogance of a man consumed with only his right to rule. "Who said anything about love?" he threw back at her. "Duty. She is my mistress. And as for my appetite," his gaze trawled over her in carnal appreciation, "I am insatiable!"

She shuddered as a wave of sensation swamped her protests. She loathed the power he held over her.

"You are not a mere pawn, *habibti*. Contrary to what you may think, I care about what happens to my son's mother. *Unlike my father.* I can't change the past. But I can change the future."

He stopped in front of a giant contemporary building the size of an aircraft hanger. "I do not want my son marinated in fear and hatred," he said, gesturing to her belly. "I want him to feel love. So given you don't feel love for me, and nor I for you—" he said, flinging open the doors and leading her into the giant space. "It's yours. Do with it as you wish."

Lucy had heard of oil-rich Arabs handing fantastic gifts to people who had won their favor. She knew such gifts generated a sense of obligation upon the person who received them. But he already owned her. At least, that was what he believed. So that made his motive what? Her mind lapped great circuits of possibility as she took in the vast space painted gallery-white, with high ceilings fitted with spotlights.

"Three months," he said.

What was he asking of her?

"You have twelve weeks before the child is born to fill this space with your new collection."

"What collection?" she lobbied.

"The collection of paintings you will create to honor the birth of my heir. The collection of paintings that I will ensure the world's wealthiest art collectors flock to view when they pay my son and me their respects. The collection of paintings that I guarantee will sell by word of mouth alone."

Despite her anger, she felt a delicious thrill of excitement as she visualized the successful accomplishment of the audacious quest he was dangling before her. Then gulped as realization dawned. Was he trying to buy her affection? *Again*?

It was so confusing.

"So you see, already you're mistaken. I do not plan to destroy your career. I plan to lift you to stratospheric heights of fame. You are insanely gifted. It would be wrong to allow your talent to languish while you are here."

One moment, he was saying she could do what she wished in the space, and the next, he was bossing her around like an autocratic ruler.

"I couldn't possibly create the number of paintings such a vast space would demand."

"You can and you will."

"I appreciate your faith in me," Lucy reluctantly conceded. "But, I don't know where to begin," she said, her eyes falling on the giant blank canvases stacked in a corner of the gallery space. "I don't know what to paint."

"*Feelings*," Anwar said. "You will paint feelings."

"*Feelings*?" she said incredulously. Right now, she didn't know what she felt. On the one hand, she felt absurdly happy at receiving the perfect gift, a studio and gallery of her own, large enough to hang paintings ten stories high.

On the other, she felt bewilderment at the enormity of the task that Anwar deemed so simple. Then, there was the turmoil of confusion about what she should be feeling. Should she be angry with Anwar for kidnapping her? He had treated her so badly. Should she marinate in the hurt his past actions had inflicted?

She raked her hands through her hair. Her mind was muddled. Nothing made any sense. Was this his love language? Instead of telling her he was sorry, was he trying to buy his way to redemption? Lucy didn't know what she felt.

Every time she looked at him, all she saw was a waterfall of tears born of love and war.

"No one has ever made a phone call on my behalf, opened any doors, or given me any favors," she threw at him. "Until you." Anger and hurt tainted her normally measured voice. "I always hated the idea of carrying the burden of people saying I only got where I am because of who I slept with. Until now, everything I achieved has been on my own merit. But now you are ruining it. You're ruining everything," Lucy said defiantly. "*I never should've slept with you.*"

"So I see," his eyes sparkled as he glanced at her belly.

She wanted to tell him, 'You left a hole in my heart when Hamad falsely accused me of art fraud, and you didn't believe me. You walked away from helping me, and my heart followed you out the door.'

She massaged her belly in fluid, soothing, circular movements. On one thing, they did agree. Babies were supposed to be born of love. She knew that how she felt while her son was in her womb would have a lifelong impact on him. Her baby would develop in a peaceful, nurturing environment if she felt happy and calm. So that meant what? Forgiveness? Absolution? Exoneration?

Should she try and forgive Anwar? Should she refuse to look back in anger? Should she fake it until she makes it—learning to love Anwar and her time of captivity? If not for her, then for her son to ensure he had the best possible start and an enduring future?

CHAPTER TWELVE

He spent a good deal of time researching narcissistic abuse survivor syndrome to try to understand better Lucy's scars. As far as he could tell, being emotionally abused by a narcissist leads a person down either of two paths. They either adopted narcissistic traits themselves, or they were a survivor who made the world a better place with love, compassion and kindness. Lucy had proven she was no liar, and he decided he would make it up to her.

He had discovered that the best way to help someone recovering from narcissistic abuse syndrome was to encourage self-care. This was essential for their healing and well-being. One of the best cures was encouraging a person in recovery to engage in activities they love and that bring them joy. Lucy loved to paint, and they both knew the healing that art could bring. While he was no painter, Lucy was, and he gained unexpected happiness knowing he had found the perfect way to encourage her to paint her way to healing.

. . .

She looked like someone releasing her inner firepower, Anwar thought as he watched her in the studio several days later.

Her red silk kaftan flowed around her like rivulets of molten lava as she hurled paint at the canvas. She was clearly impatient to unleash whatever emotions were pent inside. She didn't bend her concern to the expensive dress he had purchased for her, or care whether it was splattered with paint. The dress was one of many clothing items he had procured for her since she arrived. Whatever made her happy, he mused, cognisant she was in the last trimester of her pregnancy.

Sprays of color infused the image like clouds blowing steam and vapor, rising from the sea like molten hot lava contacting the water. Anwar scratched his head. What was she painting? Was Lucy channeling the volcanic eruption In New Zealand that she had told him had nearly claimed her friend Kate Millar's life one Christmas? Or was she painting the vibrant fireworks displayed when Kate and her lover Gianni Romano married on the volcanic island of Stromboli? Whatever the motivation, Lucy's passions were aroused.

What is soft is strong, Anwar mused as he watched whirls of water-infused paint create crashing waves on the giant canvas. Lucy thrust a sizeable flat paintbrush into a bucket of paint at her feet, then gripping the handle tightly, thrust the brush in rapid staccato movements toward the painting.

Arms outstretched, Lucy continued splashing paint around as the volcano erupted in the distance. The expression on her face was strong, unsmiling, and somewhat stern.

In the foreground, he could see an abstract rendering of the oasis of lush palm trees and tropical flowers flourishing in Avana's hot and humid environment. Three falcons swooped down from overhead, their fanned feathers catching glints of gold from the volcanic eruption in the distance and the radiant rays of the falling sun.

It was as though she was also imagining herself on a tropical island, looking out to sea. Is that where she yearned to be, he wondered, not here with me? Was Lucy freeing trapped emotions arising from her resentment of him that she wanted to release?

The painting was allowing all Lucy's repressed feelings to surface, Anwar decided as he continued to watch her, entranced by her passion. She summoned her breath from the depths of her lungs and exhaled quickly as though she was breathing out red-hot dragon fire. Anwar couldn't escape the thought that she was thinking of him and all the unresolved anger she felt towards her captor.

Or was she releasing her red, hot anger and transforming it into a willingness to love and forgive? Anwar found himself wishing it was the latter. He didn't want them to be at war. He wanted to live and love in peace.

*Love? Was that what he wanted, h*e realized with a shock.

If he and Lucy remained distant, what future did they have? He didn't want a loveless marriage like his parents, he conceded, as he watched her.

Lucy stood back and gazed at the painting for a few minutes, then settled on the ground before the canvas and closed her eyes.

Perhaps they would find a peaceful solution to their disagreement. He knew that when people suppress their feelings instead of calmly and firmly stating their needs, emotions can become pent up and blast out like an uncontrollable ball of fire. Or, worse, unexpressed feelings develop into physical issues and illness.

Hadn't he repressed his emotions all his life? He needed to take his time and think things through before reacting. He needed to try harder not to hold onto disagreements and practice forgiveness for himself and others.

Perhaps Lucy was right when she accused him of too readily believing the worst of her.

CHAPTER THIRTEEN

"Have you ever been in love, Anwar?" Lucy asked hopefully, one evening as they sat under a canopy of stars outside her studio.

"I don't need love. I have Zephyr," Anwar said.

"Zephyr is a bird."

"He has been a more loyal friend to me than anyone who professed their love." Anwar's legs spread wide, staking his claim.

"A better companion than all those women you bedded?"

"Yes," Anwar confided. "*All of them.*"

"That's because, unlike your other birds, your feathered friend doesn't talk back, and he doesn't make demands," Lucy said.

"Why are you criticizing me?"

"I'm not. I get it. That's what I'm saying."

"Why don't you speak plainly?"

"With Zephyr, you can express your emotions. Anger and sadness. Please don't deny it. I've heard the way you speak to him."

"You think that's foolish," Anwar said.

"No, I don't. Zephyr saved your sanity. Zephyr saved your life. Art is my Zephyr," she said. "My escape. My way of flying free. My way of living vicariously, soaring through rainbow clouds of color high above my life's bleak, derelict terrain. Art allows me to create landscapes of beauty, peace, and joy in my mind. I could become like a flower blossoming in the desert or a dark, dank swamp. Art enables me to find fertile ground and refuge within my creativity whenever the storm clouds blow."

"We lived in crisis mode, you and I, didn't we? As children, we learned how to be alone. Being alone seemed tidier," Anwar confided. "Except I wasn't alone. I had Zephyr."

"But it's not enough. It was never enough. That's why we've come together. I can see that now to help each other. To heal," Lucy said.

"I don't need help."

"But you do. We all do. You're not comfortable accepting help, Anwar. You've learned that it's easier to give than to receive. So you shower people with expensive gifts and coveted positions. But, like the arid landscape of your heart, despite being so thirsty, you've forgotten that you need gifts to water your soul, too. *The gift of a woman's love.*"

"And you, *habibti?*" Anwar said, steering the conversation away from the uncomfortable truth.

"I need you. All of you, Anwar. Not your money, not your title, not your gifts. I need your love. I'm beyond thankful for the time bringing me to Avana has given me. And for this beautiful space in which to create," Lucy said, sweeping her arm around the once-empty room full of new memories and stories of a brighter future.

"The studio is so symbolic of us. It's like a portal, offering a powerful window of closure, releasing what was and moving into new time and space. Once, it was like a big, vast blank canvas, waiting to be filled with something new."

She studied Anwar's expression as his eyes savored all the memories. His gaze drifted to the painting she had created last night. Waves of swirling magenta and pulsing violet danced with life on the giant canvas still drying on the floor.

"Looking over the past can bring up nostalgia but also heartfelt gratitude and, of course, trigger uncomfortable feelings around things we would rather forget. But we can allow more space for just being and loving instead of the distracting and distancing that happens when we spend too much time escaping into doing. I am beyond thankful for your encouragement and support. You're teaching me that to change, grow, and expand my life, I need to accept help lovingly. And you're giving that to me. I'm so self-reliant, so used to being let down, you're restoring my faith."

She turned to him, searching his face for any sign of softening. "Now, I would like to give you that gift. Will you let me help you? Will you tear down your fortress, all those impenetrable walls and barricades you've erected around your heart?"

His shoulders flared back.

"Will you let me love you?" Gosh, what was she saying? She didn't even know if she could go through the pain of disappointment again, but she wanted to try. And if that meant faking it until she made it, fine. *Keep your eye on the prize.*

His head lowered.

"It's not weak."

Anwar's shoulders slumped. A giant knot of air escaped his chest.

"True growth always involves some loss. Loss of the old self," Lucy said, wrapping her arms around him. "To

63

encourage growth on a tree, we prune away dead and broken branches," she whispered. "The broken parts of you. The boy who was abandoned and terrorized by his father hardened his heart so he could endure everything. It's time to let the memories go," she said, stepping toward him. "Toss them to the desert and the stars and let love in."

It was supposed to be his job to heal her, not the other way around. How the hell could he let love in when he had spent his whole life building a fortress to keep the unpredictable out? It was more than he could fathom.

He had always been the one showering others with gifts and offering his help. It was his way of expressing the affection he could not fully reciprocate. He was acutely aware that beneath his generous exterior lay scars of past experiences that had left him emotionally scarred.

When confronted with the notion of allowing love to enter his heart, Anwar froze. He longed to experience the depths of love, to let Lucy in and be vulnerable, but the fear of being hurt again paralyzed him. He could have told her that he had become adept at giving, at pouring his heart into helping others, as it was a way to shield himself from the potential pain that love could bring.

Instead, he bent his will to what he could control, shutting Lucy out.

CHAPTER FOURTEEN

"My life was nothing but drawings and dreams once," Melanie said, entering Lucy's studio. "Wow, these are hot with emotion. I love them," she said as she studied the collection. 'The rhythm, the composition, the color—they're like a magical musical score."

"That's kind of you to say."

"Not at all. It's what I feel. You've got an amazing ability to capture emotion. It's so cool to see you finally following your passion!"

Melanie stared at the canvas Lucy had just been putting the final strokes on. A vibrant, pulsating field of colors in contrasting combinations of fiery reds, lush greens, and earthy browns.

"Wow! There's so much energy in your work. I love these dynamic, gestural brushstrokes!" Melanie stepped closer to the painting until she was only centimeters away, then turned to Lucy. "It's great to see you back."

"It wasn't by choice," Lucy said.

"I know the feeling," Melanie confided. "I was a reluctant bride once."

"It was different for you. You weren't being blamed for something you didn't do."

"That's true, but nobody wanted me here. Least of all, Tariq."

"You got married. What changed between you?"

"Giving love a second chance." Melanie glanced at the scatter of canvases splayed across the studio floor and smiled. "I always wanted to paint," she said.

"Why don't you?"

"*Fear,*" Melanie paused as though considering how much to reveal. "Fear I'll make a mistake. Which is silly, really. I know it's only paint. I mean, it's not like a massively over-scaled building where one misplaced measurement can put the whole thing in jeopardy. I think it's mostly fear of beginning again. I don't want to start something new. I'm good at architecture."

"You're *great* at architecture!" Lucy corrected.

"That's the thing, Lucy. *You and Anwar are great together.* At least you were *before* Hamad did what he did."

"You were the only one who stood up for me."

"I had to. I knew it was wrong. I couldn't remain silent. But then, it's easier for me."

"Easier?" Lucy threw. "No way. That took balls."

Melanie grinned. "There are pros and cons of being the outsider in Avana. The Westerner. The import. You're freer to say what you think and feel. You never truly belong. It's almost expected that you won't conform."

"I hadn't thought of it that way," Lucy said.

"It's different for the na Hassir brothers. Their relationship is difficult. Strained. Dysfunctional. But they love each other."

"They have a crazy way of showing it."

"Show me a family that doesn't," Melanie said. "Look at the British Royals."

"Princess Diana would be so upset," Lucy agreed. "Harry and Wills don't talk anymore. It's so sad."

"The trouble is there are too many voices in their ears, meddling, manipulating, mixing truth with lies, feuds with friendship, sickness with health. Then there's their father's legacy. He instilled competition and rivalry between his children, then twisted it with a code of loyalty at all costs. Hamad's accusation tested Anwar's loyalty. The na Hassir family had to come first. He didn't want what happened to Harry and Wills to happen to his family."

"Why are you telling me this?"

"Family is everything, but they're damaged," Melanie said. "Anwar is scarred. But he wants to start a family. A happy family. He wants a lineage of his own, untainted by the past. And you are the woman he wants to do this with. You will always be first."

"He barely acknowledges me," Lucy studied the floor of the studio. "Not romantically, anyway."

"Give him time."

"He's made it clear. Three months. That's all the time I've got. Drop the baby and then bugger off."

"He said that?"

"Not exactly."

"He's repressed. They all are. *Or were.* They hold onto grievances, distract themselves with veiled indifference, and bury themselves in work."

"Sounds like me," Lucy conceded.

"And me," Melanie laughed. "Architecture was my big love. *My only love once.* Work kept my guilt, anger, and shame at bay. I kept the truth about my baby, *our baby*, from Tariq and gave Salim away."

"You gave Salim to your sister to care for. Tariq's older brother raised him as his own. It's not like you gave your son to some random stranger."

"Tariq didn't see it that way. Not at first," Melanie said. "He only met his son when Salim was three years old. Tariq was furious. You were always going to keep your baby."

"You had your reasons," Lucy said.

Melanie nodded. "Yes, I did," she said softly. "As no doubt did you. Anwar values loyalty above all else. It matters to him deeply that you were going to keep his child. He's hurt that you didn't tell him…that you were going to keep your pregnancy a secret."

"After how he treated me? How could I forgive him? How could I risk telling him of our child? I didn't know what he would do. He might have expelled me from his life permanently, taken the boy, and never let me see my child. Anything could've happened."

"He had to let you go. Anwar believed Hamad. The evidence was compelling."

"But you didn't."

"Women's instinct and intuition," she said. "And my rational mind wasn't clouded with family duty and misplaced loyalties. Anwar may be many things, but he is not heartless."

"No. A heartless man would not love a falcon as he does," Lucy said.

"It's a surrogate for the real thing," Melanie said. "A woman he can trust. A woman he can love."

Lucy sucked in a breath and swept her hands brusquely over the rivulets of painted molten lava she had hurled at the canvas. "I can't forgive him." She pressed her palms firmly and smeared a blaze of red along the length of the artwork.

"I know. I know," Melanie said softly. "When Tariq abandoned me, it hurt so much I felt like my heart was burning. I wanted marriage. I wanted a man who would love me. I wanted children. He didn't. Not to a commoner. At least, that was what his advisors decreed. I vowed never to open myself to pain like that again. It was beyond horrific—the worst of circumstances. I wanted to flee from the tainted memories that united us and stained our past. I wanted to run from the contamination of the choices I had made. I wanted to bolt from the danger Tariq presented. But imagine if I hadn't given our love a second chance?"

"You wouldn't have your beautiful children," Lucy said

"Yes, and I wouldn't be happily married to a man who loves and adores me and encourages my career."

"Anwar's been very supportive of my art. More supportive than my mother or father or anyone I loved."

"I know. He showed me the collection he purchased. He's your biggest fan. I can see why," Melanie said, sweeping her hands around the studio.

"What can I do?"

"Trust the hand of fate that has brought you together again. Trust the love that has created your child. Trust in the desert and its dreams. Can you do that?"

* * *

When Anwar employed Lucy, Lucy Gaysford, as she was then known, as his art expert, the kingdom was aflame with the news that Tariq's younger brother had hired a foreigner to acquire rare pieces of art on the kingdom's behalf. A foreigner! A Westerner! An outsider! The kingdom reeled. But behind closed doors Melanie clapped and smiled and whooped with joy.

She knew too well what it was like to be an outsider. Neither a member of the boy's club nor the gender or class deemed most worthy. Secretly, she always cheered for the underdog, except she knew Lucy was no one to be underestimated. Her credentials and achievements aside, Melanie sensed Lucy had an inner talent, a source of genius that perhaps even Lucy never knew she possessed. It took an artist to see an artist, she reflected as she gazed around her studio.

Melanie had watched with admiration and pleasure as Lucy convinced Anwar to break with stuffy tradition, encouraging him to acquire extraordinary contemporary artworks for his collection. Rothko's, Pollocks, Twomblys, de Koonings, and more—all male artists Melanie noted to her dismay, arrived from America, Europe and Asia.

The people of Avana were horrified. "What is this rubbish?" "My 3-year-old son could have painted better," in the wake of scorching criticism, Lucy remained steadfast—with Anwar's unwavering support.

Melanie admired Lucy's bravery and daring and her influence. She had always thought Anwar's priceless collection of 15th-century master paintings was too safe, too somber, too stuffy—better suited to crusty old shrines to the past than a region embracing the future.

Sadly, it was inevitable that with Lucy's considerable talent came envy. People, all anonymous, hiding in the shadows of secrecy, set out to discredit Lucy. Melanie could have hazarded a guess who, starting with the former art consultant that Anwar had fired when he passed full control of his collection to Lucy.

In those early months that Lucy worked with Anwar, Melanie had hoped that she would soon have an ally, a friend, a confident, another woman from the West she could confide in—and dreamed of collaborating on some design project in the future. But that was not to be.

As quickly as Lucy arrived, she disappeared in a malström of brutal, career-ending accusations and shame. It had been at Melanie's insistence that Anwar went in search of her.

"Bring her back. Reveal the truth. Or are you afraid?" Melanie had goaded.

Melanie knew very well what Anwar feared. All na Hassirs were the same. They feared love because they had been raised to hate.

Women's intuition and instinct, plus a good ground to the ear, told Melanie that Anwar and Lucy's connection ran deeper than a working relationship. She had heard the rumors, firmly suppressed by the palace, that one night, when the desert was rich with dreams, Anwar had stolen Lucy's heart.

One night, when the desert dreamed, Anwar had lowered the triple-plated, fortified barriers around his heart. One night, when the desert dreamed, Lucy and Anwar had made love. And that was as wonderful as it was dangerous.

People who coveted Anwar's position, his wealth, and his title were firmly opposed to his happiness—and Allah forbid it, an heir! Melanie would not, could not let the forces of hateful darkness steal love and light again.

CHAPTER FIFTEEN

In a world enamored with lies, flowers always told the truth, Anwar reflected as he entered his private sanctuary—a hidden paradise where his love for orchids bloomed. As the sun cast its golden rays upon the tranquil garden, the Sheikh strolled amidst a kaleidoscope of vibrant petals, his troubled heart filling with solace and joy.

He nurtured each delicate orchid with meticulous care, whispering words of encouragement as he tended to their needs. His fingers gently caressed the smooth, glossy leaves, his touch a testament to his deep connection with the exquisite flowers.

Surrounded by a symphony of fragrances, Anwar's thoughts were momentarily distracted from the predicament Lucy and he now faced. He bent his face to the flowers and inhaled, delighting in the unique scent of each orchid variety. From the intoxicating vanilla notes of the Vanda Miss Joaquim to the delicate floral aroma of the Phalaenopsis, his senses were captivated by nature's perfumed masterpieces. Their beauty stirred his soul, transporting him to a realm of serenity.

His thoughts drifted to Lucy and how similar she was to the orchids he loved. Delicate, yet strong. Fragile, yet enduring. Independent, yet needing protection. Had he done the right thing by abducting Lucy— stealing her away from her life, her friends, and her family?

Family! Predators and traitors! Wasn't that the lesson his brutal upbringing instilled in him, he mused as his laser vision narrowed on tiny aphids burrowed within the leaves of his precious flowers? The tenacious vultures hung in the shadows, sucking all that was good and beautiful. Just like his family. Just like Lucy's family.

But it didn't have to be this way, he affirmed as he scraped the aphids with his fingertips and squashed them resolutely. Lucy and his unborn child were his family now. He would do everything possible to protect those most precious to him. No matter the personal cost, he would provide Lucy and his son with a love-filled future.

Anwar moved slowly through the giant, climatically controlled glass house, studying the intricate patterns of the orchids' petals, marveling at how nature painted such uniquely intricate designs, each with its own DNA. With a keen eye for detail, he had identified the specific conditions required for each orchid's optimal growth—temperature, humidity, and sunlight—ensuring they flourished under his watchful gaze.

If he could do this for his flowers, why couldn't he achieve this for Lucy? She felt like her freedom had been stolen by the sheikh. But in time, she would see how they would all flourish. That much he could, and *would,* control.

Anwar tore his thoughts away as his servants approached. He waved them away and reached for the hose, insisting on watering the orchids himself. As tiny droplets of water sprayed over the blooms, he marveled at the resilience and diversity of the fragile plants. Each one held a story, a unique journey of growth and survival.

Flowers taught him patience as he waited for the lime green buds carrying new life to unfold. And they taught him humility as he witnessed their blossoming and beheld the grandeur of their unreplicable beauty.

His love for orchids was not only a personal passion but a symbol of his dedication to preserving the natural treasures of Avana and rescuing rare species at risk of extinction. Through his private greenhouse, he sought to educate others about the miraculous world of orchids, inspiring them to appreciate the delicate balance between man and nature. His passion for orchids married perfectly with art—each created beauty, blossoming in a world that seemed enamored with ugliness and hate.

Unlike paintings, his flowers could not be faked. His thoughts drifted to the accusation lobbied against Lucy by his brother, Hamad. For a brief moment, in his oasis of tranquillity, Anwar found respite from the trappings of greed and deceit and the demands of his royal duties. Here, amid the whispering leaves and gentle hum of bees, he could escape and find solace in the simplicity of nature's wonders.

His thoughts drifted to Lucy again. She was his reluctant bride. It shouldn't matter, but it did. Why did her refusal to submit ache so? Was it time to let the buds of love unfold and open his heart to the beauty in her belly soon to flower?

His unborn child rested in the sacred waters of his mother's womb. New life was unfolding within the nurturing cocoon of her sacred body. It was a big responsibility. *Would he get it right and be a great dad or fuck it up as his parents had?* He lowered his face to the fragrant magenta-coloured orchid and raked his hand through his hair. He was going to be a father.

"New life will soon be here," he whispered to the orchids. "The start of a new cycle." Anwar looked around the greenhouse. "I'll be honest," he whispered when he was sure he was alone. "I've led legions of armies into battle, conquered warlords and despots, slayed tyrants and dictators, but this role is my greatest challenge yet. To be a good father. To sire a strong and noble son. To lead a child into manhood. This I have never done."

He hesitated. "I feel. . .dare I admit it. . . uncertain. The world has gone mad," he said, turning to his beloved white orchids. White, the color of peace, he reflected. Usually, the ivory blooms made him feel calm. Why did he suddenly feel so unsettled?

"*I'm afraid I'll fuck it all up,*" he admitted.

Was that why he pushed Lucy away? Was it easier to intentionally sabotage their relationship than put his whole heart into the game and discover he was a failure?

An A+ failure at love. An A+ failure as a husband. An A+ failure as a dad.

What if his father was right? Anwar thought as he pulled dead leaves from his plants. He had been a total failure as a son. His father had said he was a waste of space, not worth the title and vast wealth he had inherited.

No, Anwar corrected, snipping a dead bloom with sharp scissors. My father was a fatally flawed man. If Anwar was a fuck up in his father's eyes, it was because of his dysfunctional cruelty. Anwar had been neglected, starved of love, and beaten with cold indifference, just like the cruelty Lucy had been subjected to as a child. Was that what drew him to return to New York to find her? Was that why he was so resolute in keeping her here?

I was innocent once, untainted by my family's reign, he silently acknowledged. His unborn child was still an untainted innocent. He deserved happiness. *They all deserved happiness*, he vowed.

"It feels daunting," Anwar admitted as he gently misted the orchids' leaves with water. Rainbow light danced off the droplets like tiny mirrors, Anwar mused, reflecting what was to come. New life. New memories. A new beginning.

Don't be so hard on yourself, Anwar silently affirmed. Ease into your new role as a father and a husband. Learn to gently release the past and make space for this time of magical renewal.

He would ensure infinite love always surrounded his child and his wife, he vowed, casting an appreciative glance around his beloved beauties before heading back to the palace. And he knew just the place to start.

CHAPTER SIXTEEN

What if life could be easier, Lucy wondered? What if all she had to do was cede her fierce self-reliance and allow herself to accept Anwar's protection—even if he couldn't, or wouldn't love her?

Lucy tightened all the lids on her buckets and tubes of paint, washed her brushes, and stepped outside the studio as the sun dipped below the horizon, casting a fiery glow over the rolling desert dunes. Could she follow Melanie's advice and trust in the desert and its dreams? Giving love a second chance had worked for her and Tariq. Could it work for Lucy and Anwar? What she needed was a sign.

Her gaze soared upward as a male and female falcon took flight, their mighty wings slicing through the balmy evening air. The unmistakable grace and elegance of their aerial dance captivated her attention.

The male, a regal creature with shimmering chestnut feathers, soared effortlessly through the sky, his wings spread wide as if embracing the very essence of freedom. His sharp eyes, gleaming with determination, scanned the landscape below for any sign of prey. He exuded an unmatched sense of purpose and poise with each beat of his wings.

Beside him, the female falcon, a vision of beauty with her sleek, sable plumage, matched his every move. Her wings, as dark as the night sky, contrasted against the fading light, creating a mesmerizing display of contrasting hues. Her gaze, intense and focused, mirrored her mate's unwavering determination.

As they circled higher, their flight path became a delicate ballet. Each twist and turn was executed with precision and grace, their bodies moving in perfect synchrony. It was as if they were connected by an invisible thread, guiding their every movement. Lucy's thoughts drifted to Anwar and the night they had spent together when their son was conceived. She found herself yearning to experience feeling bound together, not in lust but love, she affirmed as she glanced again at the falcons.

The wind whispered through the trees, carrying a sense of ancient wisdom as the falcons continued their celestial waltz. They seemed to defy gravity, effortlessly gliding through the currents with confidence and mastery. Lucy watched transfixed as their flight patterns changed in unison, as if communicating a secret language known only to them. The male falcon, ever the protector, took the lead, scouting ahead for any potential threats. His wings pulsed with a purposeful rhythm, propelling him forward with astonishing speed.

The female falcon, ever watchful, followed closely behind her male companion, her eyes keenly scanning the landscape. Her slightly smaller but no less powerful wings moved with an elegance that belied her strength. She was a formidable hunter in her own right, her focus unyielding. They were true partners and equals, harmonizing with each other's weaknesses and strengths.

How she envied their love, Lucy told herself. It was the relationship of equals she sincerely wanted.

As the fading sun cast a golden hue over the landscape, the falcons swooped lower, their flight path curving towards a cluster of Frankincense trees. With a swift movement, the male falcon veered to the right, his sharp eyes honed in on a movement below the fragrant bushes—a *potential target*.

The female falcon, sensing his intent, mirrored his trajectory. Together, they descended upon their unsuspecting prey, their talons outstretched, ready to strike. With a burst of speed, they closed in, their wings tucked tightly against their bodies.

In a breathtaking display of precision and skill, the male falcon swooped down, his talons finding their mark. The female falcon followed suit, her aim just as accurate. Together, they captured their prey, their feathers ruffling in the gust of their descent.

With their meal secured and their terrain protected, the falcons ascended again, their wings carrying them higher into the vast expanse of the evening sky. In their triumphant flight, they seemed to embody the essence of freedom and power, a reminder of fierce poise in the natural world.

Inspiration struck as they circled ever higher, their silhouettes fading into the twilight. There was no reason to spend her time in Avana pointlessly—just the opposite.

CHAPTER SEVENTEEN

T he next evening, as the sun painted the sky with hues of gold and crimson, Lucy found herself alone in her studio. Zephyr perched on a nearby branch, his piercing gaze fixed upon her. She could sense an unspoken message in his eyes, as if urging her to explore her creative potential.

Lucy's artistic spirit burned brighter as renewed inspiration struck. Wouldn't it be beautiful to paint Anwar's beloved bird?

She knew that capturing the essence of such a magnificent creature would be a challenge, yet she embraced it with unwavering enthusiasm. With a palette of vibrant pigments and a collection of carefully crafted brushes, she was determined to immortalize the falcon's beauty. With each brush stroke, she sought to convey the falcon's grace, strength, and the untamed spirit that coursed through its veins.

She found inspiration in the earth itself, gathering pigments from the desert's sands, where hues of ochre, sienna, and burnt umber lay waiting to be transformed into art. She meticulously ground the pigments, infused them with her creative energy, and mixed them with her handcrafted oils, blending them to create the perfect hues and textures.

As Lucy worked, the desert wind whispered in her ear, carrying fragments of stories and legends. It spoke of Anwar, whose benevolence and love for nature were known far and wide. Lucy wanted to present her falcon masterpiece as a gift to Anwar, a peace offering reflecting her gratitude for his belief in her talent, the desert's beauty, and the falcon's enchanting presence that had fired her creativity.

With each brushstroke, Lucy poured her heart into the canvas. She meticulously recreated the falcon's fiery eyes, capturing their piercing gaze that seemed to hold the secrets of the desert. The intricate patterns of the falcon's feathers danced across her canvas, their delicate details a testament to the divine craftsmanship of nature.

Days turned into nights, nights into days, as Lucy's dedication to her art consumed her. Sometimes, she painted at night, taking her easel outside and painting beneath the celestial canopy, the twinkling stars bearing witness to her creative journey. The desert, her muse, whispered encouragement, guiding her hand as she breathed life into the falcon's portrait.

Finally, after countless hours of unwavering focus, Lucy stepped back to observe her masterpiece. Frozen in time on the canvas, the falcon seemed to come alive with a vitality that mirrored the essence of its existence. She marveled at her creation, knowing it would be a cherished offering for Anwar.

Her heart brimmed with anticipation as she presented her artwork to Anwar. "I wanted to create something special, someone special," she corrected. "To hang in your office, perhaps," she suggested. "My mother wanted a portrait of her grandmother because she loved her the most. And you love Zephyr the most."

She held her breath, waiting for his reaction, remembering as she did the stony silence that suffocated the joy she had felt in giving her mother the portrait she had painted. Would he think it was a silly present, unworthy of a prince with so much wealth?

Anwar was speechless as he took hold of Lucy's painting. A wave of reverence washed over him as he gazed at the falcon. The canvas seemed to pulsate with an energy that resonated deep within his soul. Gently tracing the intricate brushstrokes with his fingers, he marveled at her ability to capture the essence of the falcon's spirit.

In that moment, he was transported back to his childhood, when he would escape his father's brutality and wander the desert, feeling the sand beneath his feet and the wind caressing his face. The falcons had always held a special place in his heart, symbolizing happiness, freedom, and the untamed beauty of the natural world.

The more he gazed at the painting, the more Anwar saw more. It was not just a stunning portrayal of a falcon. He saw Lucy's devotion, her unwavering commitment to capturing a fleeting moment of nature's magnificence and celebrating the majesty of the falcon he so loved. The layers of pigment and the delicate blending of oils spoke of her dedication, not just to her craft, but to him. It was a selfless gift, given only to make him happy.

What to do? What to say? Anwar wondered. He understood the significance of this gift, not only as a physical object and as a representation of the interconnectedness of all things but as a truce. An unspoken agreement between enemies to stop fighting. For a specific time. But how long would it last? Lucy was not here willingly, even if she was determined to make the most of her time in captivity.

"Your gift—nobody has ever given me anything so beautiful and personal."

"Do you really like it?"

"Like it? I love it! My heart is full," Anwar said. "It truly is a masterpiece. It's not just a painting, is it?"

"What do you mean?"

"It is a profound expression of love and respect for Zephyr, the desert, and its inhabitants."

Lucy nodded. "I wanted to embody everything special to you."

"And you have. I will cherish it forever and hang it in a place of honor within my palace, where its presence will inspire all who see it."

Her gaze drifted to the floor as heat flamed her cheeks. Anwar smiled inwardly, knowing she found compliments hard to believe. But he also knew that an essential part of healing from narcissistic abuse was to receive heart-felt compliments and acknowledgment of her talent. Her mother and siblings had endlessly criticized and shamed her. He had read it took seven positive words to counteract a negative comment. Words were more than just letters strung together. They are the building blocks of self-image, self-worth, self-talk, and sabotaging mindsets. He wanted to grow in her confidence and appreciate her incredible worth.

"Your unique style and creativity shine through in every brushstroke," he added. "It's so beautiful. I love it. Thank you for painting it. You are a wonderful woman and artist."

The edges of her mouth flickered into a smile and then disappeared. "You're allowed to bask in your achievements, Lucy."

She lifted her head and gazed directly at him. "Thank you, Anwar."

He was heartened that his sentiments had touched her

profoundly. Her gift had no motive—only a desire to please him. It touched him more deeply than anything in his life. Was that what love for a woman felt like? The uncertainty unsettled him. Had he fallen head over toes in love with Lucy despite his fearful reluctance and fear of failure?

CHAPTER EIGHTEEN

"I've been thinking—" Anwar began. Were things between them destined always to be tense, he mused, registering Lucy's wide-eyed apprehension? "I know things haven't been easy."

"*Easy?* You mean snatching me from my life in New York and depositing me here was meant to be easy?"

"No, not that. The thing with Hamad."

"The *thing*!" She repeated. "The thing being Hamad's false accusation? *The thing* you so readily believed? *The thing* that destroyed my career?"

"Yes, that thing," he said, not wanting to dredge up the past and dignify the unfortunate chain of events with concrete details of the fraud of which Lucy had been accused. Instead, he wanted to put energy into healing the wounds that defined them both. "I want to put things right."

"And just how do you plan to do that?"

"I want your continued expertise as my art advisor."

The truth was they needed each other. He respected her skills, and appointing her to this critical role would show Lucy and her detractors that she deserved respect.

"You are joking!"

"I need you, and that's not going to change."

It never went away. Every time I see your face, the feeling is the same as the first day I saw you. My love of art, beauty, nature, it's all because of you.

"I want us to start again," Anwar said.

She looked at him. "What do you mean?"

"You have fueled my ambition."

"I have?"

"Your passion and purpose. It's how we met. It's what unites us. You have always been captivated by the artistic expressions of women throughout history, and you have always believed that their voices deserve to be heard and celebrated on a grand scale. You were pioneering and brave. I always admired that. You held that vision long before we met. But now, after seeing your collection and feeling the intensity of your work, I can see an excellent way to integrate all our passions. I need your help to give birth to a dream flaming in my heart.

Her delicate brows furrowed. "I'm confused."

"*Maerid al'ahlam. The Gallery of Dreams*," he said. "I want to create a world-class contemporary art museum dedicated solely to women artists. Some of the world's most iconic artworks aren't displayed in museums or art galleries. They reside in the private art collections of a few billionaires across the globe—industrialists, celebrities, members of royal families, and others. I need your help procuring elusive, rare works so that they are no longer buried in private vaults but brought into the light so people of all classes may enjoy the painting."

"*That's it? That's how you plan on fixing things between us?*"

"My reemploying you will send a very public signal that all is forgiven."

"Forgiven," she said flatly.

"Forgotten."

"Forgotten," she whispered. "Poof!" Just like that."

Her skeptical silence threw him.

Anwar wasn't sure what he expected. Some excitement, perhaps. Gratitude for the opportunity. But her reaction was cooly detached. No doubt she would accuse him again of buying her love and forgiveness, but his heart was in the right place, and his intention pure.

Would time ease their pain, and something beautiful would remain in its place?

* * *

"That's amazing," Maria Bright said when Lucy rang her and told her of Anwar's ambitious project. "You'll be the art world's darling with all that money to buy incredible art."

"I haven't accepted the position. Not yet."

"What? Do you need your head read? What's not to accept?"

"I'm still grieving."

"Grieving what? Who died."

"*I died*. At least a part of me did when Anwar didn't back me and walked out of my life."

"Well, he's backing you now."

"It's not the same."

"I seem to recall you telling me that you ran."

"They were going to imprison me."

"But they didn't, did they? You cleared your name."

"Mud sticks."

"But now Anwar is offering you a way to clean the sordid mess."

Lucy sighed. "Maybe."

"Look, I get it, Lucy. I do," Maria said sympathetically. "When you told me what Hamad accused you of, how hurt you'd been when Anwar believed his lies, I felt your pain. The art world is rife with scandals and betrayals. It's brutal. But that's called living in the real world. Love hurts. Life hurts. But you're a survivor. I've seen how the experience has changed you for the better. You're stronger. Smarter. Savvier. You're not the naive, trusting woman you told me you were when you first met Anwar."

Lucy smiled. "No," she conceded. "I'm a new me. Complete with baby!"

"A baby!"

"I was going to tell you. It's just—"

"You hadn't told Anwar."

"Yes. And we're married—did I tell you?"

"What? But that's amazing!"

"No, not really, " Lucy said, forelornly. "He slid a piece of paper toward me over breakfast just after we landed in Avana, told me it was our marriage contract and to sign it if I wanted our son to be legitimized."

"What did you do?"

"I told you, we're married," Lucy said flatly.

"Grief turns into the new," Maria said. "Grief of the career you thought you'd lost. Grief of events beyond your control. Grief of the love you yearned for…but it's all seeding a new future. Even if it's not how you planned things, there's still hope for miracles."

"Not where Anwar is concerned. He told me himself he doesn't believe in love. And nor do I."

"There is love in holding on, and there is love in letting go. But mostly, there is love in second chances. Anwar's showing you his love language—the studio space and now the curator position for a fabulous project. He'll come around. Besides, what's not to love about you? You're a supernova of talent and the kindest, most loving person I know. Don't let your stubborn pride keep you imprisoned in the past."

"But what if he betrays me again? What if he believes another lie someone manufactures?"

"What matters is that you know the truth. People lie, and facts tell the truth. Sooner or later, what is real will come to light. In the meantime, live in the present. Let go of your fear the past will repeat. You don't have to see the whole staircase of your future. Just take the first step in faith. Stop giving your power away. Say yes to being Anwar's curator. Can you do that?"

CHAPTER NINETEEN

"How did you give your power away?"

Lucy sat in bed and stared at a YouTube clip she had been watching on her iPad, unable to answer. It was by famous British Astrologer Lee Harris in his monthly energy update. The title had captured her attention: '*Empaths and Narcissists, a Guide to Healing Trauma.*'

Lee offered a three-part video to help recover from narcissistic abuse, but Lucy decided she didn't need to take his online course. She had enough therapy to sink a ship. What she needed to do was put what she knew into practice. Putting her phone on the bedside table, she told herself she needed her journal and paints. Recalling what her art therapist, Issy Riley, had taught her during their counseling sessions, she reached down and fetched the box of crayons and other art supplies she kept under the bed. She opened the lid and instinctively picked up a black crayon.

Black, the color of darkness, she affirmed to herself as she walked over to the desk beneath the window, placed a large A3 sheet of paper firmly down, and rapidly scribbled a thick, fierce line. Pressing more heavily as feelings she'd kept suppressed came to her mind, she drew spiraling circles like coils of graffiti.

Put some words on the page, she told herself. "I've been blind," she said out loud." She wrote, 'Blind to the narcissist's bag of tricks!'

She plunged her hand into the box and pulled out a fiery red crayon. She wrote the word 'shame'. Then, taking the flat side of the crayon, she layered washes of angry red over the black marks, staining the paper crimson.

She remembered how her face blushed horrifically when her mother teased and publicly embarrassed her with her cruel ridicule and toxic taunts. Lucy gripped the crayon in her palm and scrawled sharp zig-zags across the page, then wrote the word 'rage!'

She'd been so afraid of her mother's unpredictable outbursts of anger she learned to remain silent lest she inflamed her further. But now, free of her overbearing presence, she could express her true feelings. Feelings she had repressed for so many years.

She heaved a weary sigh and glanced at the box of colors. Her eyes were drawn to the soft, pale blue crayon almost hidden from view. She picked it up and wrote the word 'peacekeeper.'

Put some feeling words on the page, she reminded herself. 'Safe,' she wrote. Being the peacekeeper and placating others had kept her safe. Now what?

Put some help on the page, Lucy reminded herself, recalling Issy's instructions during her therapy sessions, encouraging Lucy to express the painful feelings buried in her subconscious.

She drew a white dove surrounded by angelic light. As a child, Lucy had escaped into her imagination. She lived in a world of make-believe, happy families and love-ever-afters.

She wrote stories and drew pictures of smiling animals surrounded by friends. She submitted these to competitions and won prizes, and her drawings were published in the newspaper and later in the school magazine. Lucy kept her accomplishments private because her mother would reprimand her, telling her she was showing off and being boastful and vain.

"You love yourself," her mother had said as though it was a horrible crime. "You think you're better than us."

Lucy picked up a rosy pink crayon and drew a fat, juicy heart. Then she picked up a vivid white crayon and wrote, 'I can love myself better than you ever did.'

She held the drawing up an arm's length from her face as Issy had shown her. "What else does it need?" she wondered.

'Flowers,' came the answer.

Lucy picked up her phone and scrolled through her Spotify playlist until she found Miley Cyrus. 'I can buy myself flowers,' Miley sang. As Lucy listened to the lyrics, realization dawned.

I gave my power away because I thought I needed my mother's love and approval to be lovable. I tried to be the person she wanted me to be. Quiet, always in the background, never succeeding, never flourishing, never shining, never taking her light.

Why? Because, for some perverse reason, she envied me. I took the spotlight from her, and she couldn't stand it. But why did she do that to me?

Because she was broken. Because she was deeply flawed. Because she never felt loved. Because it was easier to be nasty than sweet.

Lucy put the crayons down and walked to the window. The only things that survived in the desert's punishing environment were snakes and spiders, she mused as she glanced at the shifting sands.

Lucy suddenly remembered that at her father's funeral, despite divorcing her father 20 years prior and remarrying, her mother had complained, "What about me? Why doesn't anyone care about how I feel?" She never once asked Lucy how she felt about losing her father.

Her mother was a shape-shifting, venomous attention seeker, Lucy reluctantly conceded. Was that why Lucy shunned the spotlight? When Maria had offered her a solo exhibition, she had nearly turned it down, and now she was on the cusp of doing the same thing with Anwar's offer.

What was wrong with her?

From the day Lucy arrived in the world, she had eclipsed her mother and her siblings. They had retaliated by spraying her with their poison. Lucy didn't try to glow. She just outshone her mother naturally. People were attracted to Lucy's warmth, beauty, kindness, intelligence, and compassion. She wasn't attention-seeking. She was just born that way.

"You were always my favorite," her mother's best friend told Lucy once. "You were the best of the litter."

But the words, like all the other compliments people offered her, always washed over Lucy, landing with a splat in a giant puddle of self-doubt. Lucy bit her lips and frowned as she blinked back tears. Her mother had broken her heart and stolen her confidence and self-esteem.

But Anwar believed in her talent. He had purchased all her paintings, and then, when he could have turned a blind eye to her pregnancy, when he could have refused to recognize the child's legitimacy, when he could have cast them both aside, he determined she was worthy enough to be his wife. And now he was inviting her to co-found *Maerid al'ahlam: The Gallery of Dreams.*

Lucy pressed her lips into a determined line. She could advocate for other artists' work. She could sing their praises far and wide. She could negotiate the absolute best outcomes for others. Why couldn't she do the same for herself? Why did she always feel so unworthy?

Issy had encouraged her to collect empowering feedback and to reread it whenever her confidence needed a boost. She reached for the little journal she kept on her desk and scrolled through comments people had said to her over the years.

> *Your art speaks to my soul in a major way.*
> *Your intuitive sense of color is spectacular.*
> *Beautiful energy everywhere where you are!*
> *You are inspirational, intuitive, intelligent, creative, and loving.*

She read several more pages, then turned to her newest entry, feeling her heart tingle as she read Anwar's words.

I'm in awe.

She traced her fingers over the words and touched them to her lips, then closed the book and rose from the desk.

Maybe it's time I started believing in myself.

CHAPTER TWENTY

"Women have been underrepresented in art galleries across the globe," Lucy said. "51% of the world's official artists are women, yet they make up less than a quarter of the artists exhibited in public museums. I want to help you change that," Lucy told Anwar over dinner. "I will accept your position. I will be your curator."

"Excellent! We will make a formidable team with my wealth and your talent."

"Is that why you brought my whole collection In New York?"

"I recognized your genius. You needed someone influential to give you a start."

Lucy bit back her retort.

"It does not lessen your capability or skill," Anwar said, registering her silent protest. "It is simply reality."

She knew it was true. It wasn't what you knew. *It was who you knew*. She could draw a giant graffiti flourish in the style of Cy Twombly and struggle to find a buyer. It could be better than his work, but it would never sell for the hundreds of thousands of dollars Cy Twombly's connections had brought him. Lucy also knew that Helen Frankenthaler's success soared when she aligned with referred art critics and married the most influential of them. It would be naive and foolish to struggle on her own.

"Planning the museum will take some time. In the meantime, we will hold an exhibition to showcase your work. It will be a public display of change and solidarity. It will challenge the idea that modern and contemporary art is male-dominated. Just because they've never heard of you in the Middle East doesn't mean you are not here. You will no longer be silent, invisible, or ignored," Anwar said.

"I will do it on one condition, "Lucy said. "I want my exhibition of the works celebrating our son's arrival to be judged on their merit. The public can vote on their favorite works, and only then, if I am lucky enough to be selected to have a piece in the Gallery of Dreams, it will be because your people deemed me, *my paintings*," she corrected, "worthy."

"Very well, *habibti.* Together, with the combined synergies of the two events, we will turn up the volume. Not just on your talent, but later, when the *Maerid al'ahlam: The Gallery of Dreams* is completed, the previously unheard voices in women's art will be celebrated. And we will urge the Arabic community and other institutions to join us," he said, "Unifying our jealous neighbors and giving them something to aspire to. It's a worthy cause everyone will get behind."

Later that day, Lucy and Anwar met Melanie to discuss the building project.

"The philosophy that must guide your design for the museum in everything it does, from its foundation to the art it houses, is as a collaboration between two cultures. The dazzling architecture I know you will create will combine the best Western design with Arabic heritage."

"Other than that, you have a blank canvas—and an open checkbook," Anwar added.

"Our partnership will combine Anwar's bold vision of cultural progression and openness with your expertise in the world of architecture, " Lucy said.

"What fun," Melanie said. "We can explore the shared themes that reveal and connect art, culture, and humanity. But what of the Clerics? Have you thought how they may react?"

"There are far better things ahead than any we leave behind," Anwar said. "We will show them the value of being progressive. Where there is hope, there is a way. Art is the highest form of hope. It is time to let go of hatred and oppression. We must choose to keep our focus on that which is truly magnificent, beautiful, uplifting, and joyful. Sooner or later, we all have to let go of our past."

"Yes and no," Lucy said. "The Gallery of Dreams can't simply celebrate the present and the future, but cherish and honor the best of the past."

"Of course. If you could exhibit one painting from the past, what would it be?" Anwar asked.

"Leonardo da Vinci's Mona Lisa," Lucy said unhesitatingly. "While the painting is not by a woman artist, she is arguably the most famous woman in the world. Her portrait is so deep and mystical. In that one painting, Leonardo sought to unite the masculine and the feminine. It's so symbolic of what you stand for. Imagine if we could achieve the unattainable and get the French Government to loan The Mona Lisa for us to display at T*he Gallery of Dreams'* opening. That will never happen, but it's a lovely dream," Lucy said. "I have always loved that portrait. It's always been a dream to one day see it in person."

Anwar stood silently, his face impassive, other than the gleaming sparkles in his eyes.

CHAPTER TWENTY-ONE

"Pick up the damn phone, Hamad. Stop avoiding me!"

Anwar slammed his phone down on his desk. How the hell was he going to find the truth if his brother continued to inflame doubt?

Hamad's absence from Avana, rather than making Anwar's heart grow fonder for his recalcitrant brother, only infuriated him.

He picked up the phone and entered Fazza's number. "Where is Hamad, brother?"

There was a silent pause.

"Fazza?"

The sound of mumbled voices filtered through the airways.

"Hamad, I know you're there. Pick up!"

"Anwar," Hamad greeted his brother's command with frosty indignation.

"You've been avoiding me."

"Not at all."

Anwar heard a woman's laughter in the background.

"I've been distracted. Beautifully distracted."

"Where are you?"

"What is it you want, Anwar?"

"The truth. Hamad. I want the bloody truth!"

* * *

"Why did you believe Hamad over me?" Lucy stared hard into the pile of photos of possible art acquisitions for the museum they had met to discuss the following morning.

Surprised, Anwar leaned back and blew out a breath. "Well, that's quite a shift of topic."

"It's been on my mind. *Obviously.* Despite everything you've done to make things right, I can't forget it."

He drummed his fingers on the table. "You could say I got tired, worn down by Hamad and family pressure, but that's an excuse."

It annoyed him to admit that he realized that to be honest with Lucy was to face the truth with no excuses.

"I took the easy path. It shames me to admit it. To face the truth was too confronting. That my brother lied to me. I wanted us to be a happy family. A family that got on. I didn't want to be like my father – triangulating us, pitting us against each other. Brothers at war."

"I'm sorry, Anwar. It must have been difficult."

It was easy to see the discomfort on her face with the unhappiness of the memory, not just of his conflict with his family and yearning for love, but her painful past.

"What did any of it matter now? What was done was done. There's no need to go over it," Lucy said. "I should have let it go."

Despite everything he had done to her, she was so compassionate. So kind. *So loveable.*

"It's me who should be apologizing. You have nothing to be sorry for," he said, ignoring her desire to keep the peace. He kept his eyes locked on hers. "I always knew if anyone was fraudulent, it wasn't you. It's just—"

He frowned, looked hard at nothing, and tried to be honest again. And the answer was sad and bruising. "What we had during those brief months we spent together were the happiest, most joyous days of my life."

"Anwar," she touched his arm. He looked at the graceful hand resting on his sleeve and then recoiled as his gaze traveled to her delicate fingers.

Their marriage had been purely contractual. The only thing binding them to each other was a sheet of stiff paper and the flourish of an ink pen. He hadn't even brought her an engagement ring. He was a brute, undeserving of her forgiveness.

"You can forget many things, but can you forget love?"

"Don't," she whispered, pulling her hand away.

He'd be dammed if he'd back off. Suddenly, his entire miserable failure to love and be loved was slapped in his face.

"I'm sorry, Lucy." Those words didn't capture the depths of his remorse. Those words he knew she longed to hear slipped from his lips in a river of need and longing. "That night, that unforgettable night, we made love—"

"Sex, it was just sex," Lucy said.

"I was your first."

Her eyes were bright with anger and tears.

"Yes, you were my first," she whispered, refusing to meet his gaze.

"You were my first, too."

Her eyes flew wide.

"There had been others, of course," Anwar said.

She trembled, infuriating him and shaming him. He was hurting her. Hadn't that been why it was easier to settle for Hamad's version of the truth.

The panic came first, a chokehold that snagged air from his throat. I was afraid—afraid of what it meant. You were the first to climb into my heart and settle there."

"So you killed everything."

She was angry. She was right to be angry.

"I thought it was better to end things then. Better, when whatever we felt had just begun. . ." he struggled to find the right words, to make rational sense of the emotions that over-took him then as they were now. "I thought it was inevitable that it would end. And you were in real danger. I stepped aside."

She hugged her arms over her chest in a defensive move that sliced through his heart.

"I'm so sorry. Can you forgive me?"

When Lucy was in her room, and the lights were off, Anwar walked through the garden where he could watch her window. It wasn't so much examining the choices he made that weighed upon him but the uncertain future that awaited. Hours later, he returned alone to his bed. And when he slept, he dreamed. He dreamed of the desert and the love they had made under the stars.

CHAPTER TWENTY-TWO

Days turned into weeks, and Lucy immersed herself in the world of art and beauty as she combined her passion for painting with sourcing jaw-droppingly stunning artworks for *Maerid al'ahlam: The Gallery of Dreams.*

Anwar showered her with praise, and as she faithfully recorded his kind words in her feedback journal, she grew more confident in her abilities.

She loved her nightly catch-up with Anwar and telling him of all the paintings she and her team had found and acquired. Their conversations delved deep into the meaning behind every brushstroke, every sculpted masterpiece in both the paintings Lucy was creating and the growing collection she had procured for him.

She wondered if the creation of *Maerid al'ahlam, The Gallery of Dreams,* had always been the additional purpose of her journey to Anwar's kingdom. When he had discovered her pregnancy, Anwar had stolen her away from New York to bear his heir but also to leverage off her continued expertise as his private art advisor.

He just didn't want me *for me*, she thought forlornly. She pushed the painful thought aside and turned her thoughts to what she could control.

Known for his passion for art and his unwavering support for women's empowerment, Sheikh Anwar had a burning ambition in his heart - to create a world-class contemporary art museum dedicated solely to women artists. Despite her disappointment, she felt her admiration for him deepening during the many conversations they had where he reinforced the purpose that drove him.

As an avid art collector, Anwar had always been captivated by the artistic expressions of women throughout history. He believed their voices deserved to be heard and celebrated on a grand scale. This vision had been brewing within him for years, but now, with the resources and influence at his fingertips and Lucy beside him, he felt it was time to turn his dream into reality.

Anwar knew that creating such an audacious museum would require meticulous planning and unwavering dedication, and he knew that Lucy had the breadth of contacts to ensure its success. His faith in her was not misplaced.

She began by assembling a team of curators and art historians who shared Anwar's and Lucy's passion for procuring works by pioneering women artists.

Next, they embarked on many journeys to select a suitable location. Anwar wanted the museum to symbolize the Kingdom's commitment to art and gender equality. After careful consideration, together, they chose a prime spot overlooking the sparkling waters of the Arabian Gulf. The museum would have a commanding presence, its architecture blending seamlessly with the surrounding landscape.

Then came the task of curating an exceptional collection of artworks. Anwar agreed with Lucy that showcasing diverse women artists spanning different cultures, backgrounds, and artistic styles was essential. Lucy and her team scoured the globe, seeking hidden gems and collaborating with renowned art institutions to purchase and secure loans for iconic pieces.

In an outstanding coup, they acquired a stained glass window by Tiffany's greatest female designer. *The Garden Landscape* window was attributed to Tiffany's leading designer, Agnes Northrop, whose watercolor sketch of the central panel was also acquired for the museum's collection. The large, vibrant colored panel had been commissioned in 1912 by an American philanthropist, Sarah Cochran, who had channeled her wealth and influence into supporting women's suffrage.

"This is such a masterpiece," Lucy told Anwar. "A triple C— conceived, commissioned, and crafted by a woman."

As well as incorporating the monumental stained-glass window within the museum, the design of the building was to be a work of art in itself, inspired by organic forms and Anwar's love of orchids.

Anwar envisioned a space that would house extraordinary artworks and serve as a sanctuary for creativity and inspiration. He wanted visitors to feel a sense of awe as they entered as if stepping into the beauty of a flower and a world where women's artistic genius was celebrated and revered.

He wanted it to be contemporary and modern—with a futuristic vibe that blended seamlessly with a reverence for the past. No easy feat. But he knew Tariq's wife Melanie could meet the challenge better than anyone.

The architecture would incorporate innovative elements such as natural light-filled galleries, interactive installations, and immersive technologies to achieve this. The museum would also feature spaces dedicated to workshops, artist residencies, and educational programs, nurturing young talents and fostering community among artists and art enthusiasts alike.

The name of the museum, carefully chosen by Sheikh Anwar, was *Maerid al'ahlam: The Gallery of Dreams.* It represented his belief that dreams can become reality and that art has the power to transcend boundaries and inspire change. It was a testament to the dreams and aspirations of female artists who had often been overlooked or marginalized throughout history but refused to be silenced.

Anwar knew that to truly make a difference, the museum had to be more than just a collection of artworks. It had to be a catalyst for change, challenging societal norms and perceptions of women's artistic contributions. He envisioned the museum hosting thought-provoking exhibitions, engaging panel discussions, and collaborations with international women's organizations, amplifying the voices of women artists and empowering future generations.

In this ambitious project, at least Anwar and Lucy were kindred spirits, two people who could understand their shared passion and quest for authenticity, Anwar reflected.

Together, they sought to uncover art that spoke to the soul and could, in time, unite differing genders and cultures and change the world—ending gender apartheid for good.

CHAPTER TWENTY-THREE

Lucy's due date was now only weeks away. What if her son came early? What if she hadn't finished the body of artworks Anwar had demanded be ready to exhibit in a celebration of his son's birth?

She stared at the blank canvas. "Don't overthink it! Just do it," she said as she smeared Carmine Red straight from the tube.

It was true. Painting was exhilarating and cathartic. Just as her therapist, Issy, had told her. Art facilitated a sort of emotional bloodletting. She picked up a large brush and plunged it into a bucket of magenta, swept it over the canvas, then blended it into the red pigment with her hands. Gosh, that feels good, she mused as the paint dripped down her fingers.

The healing power of art was also one of the few things she remembered from a book she had browsed at the local library when she was small. Supposedly, it was a medieval practice that purged bad humors from your system. A kind of way to balance things out. It was a term she had always loved.

Art was her release, her bloodletting—only in a more beautiful way. Art purged all the toxicity and left only bubbles of bliss. Painting allowed her to express her anger and sorrow and free them from her soul.

When Lucy escaped her small-town upbringing in her teens, she dreamed of painting and becoming happier every time she painted. She dreamed of leaving an impact that would make other people happy, too. A legacy that would last forever in people's lives. And now, thanks to Anwar, that dream was about to come true.

She stared at her hand smeared in magenta pink. Pink as bright as the sunrise, pink like the satin ballet pumps and tutu she had worn as a child, pink the color of fairytales and romance. The magenta paint stuck to her like honey, clinging to the baggy T-shirt she loved to paint in decorated with Disney's Minnie Mouse. Mickey and Minnie were soul mates, she suddenly recalled. Like Lucy and Anwar, she hoped. She thought it would be fun to call their daughter Minnie if they had another child and she was a girl. But Anwar would never allow his son to be named after a mouse.

Lucy filled the sink with warm, soapy water and began to scrub vigorously at the paint staining her hands. Why was she so obsessed with pink? Her intellect told her that the blues, baby blue, blue like the Arabian sky, was what she should be painting. Blue was safe. Blue was for boys, but for some reason that she couldn't fathom, she didn't feel like painting blue.

But she should, she reprimanded, as she scoured her skin until it was pink and tender. Anwar was a traditionalist regarding what colors were suitable for boys.

An image of Anwar rose from the warm bubblegum pink water. She shouldn't be thinking of him, she thought as the bubbles glistened and danced, just like her stomach did as she thought of him and the child they had conceived together. A blush heated her face. That night, that exciting, totally intoxicating night. What she'd give to make love to him again.

No! Stop it. She sanctioned thrusting her hands in the water and feeling for the plug. She gripped the metal ring and wrenched it free. Her gut slopped as the water, still carrying Anwar's memory, drained away. She stared down at her bare feet. She liked to paint without shoes. Barefoot and pregnant, she laughed to herself despite her pain.

As she turned to leave, she looked back at the studio. She bunched her hair up and tied it in a scrunchie. She liked what she had achieved. She had just let go. She had let go of perfectionism and striving to figure it all out. She had let go of trying to see into the future.

She felt a wide smile lift the corners of her mouth. She liked the way the studio shimmered with wet paint. She loved how glossy it looked. She wanted to stick her fingers in the thick, glistening oil paint, scoop it all up, and eat it like cherry compote pie. Instead, she savored the texture so rich it mimicked clotted cream tinted with pink food dye.

She glanced around the oversized studio and felt her heart surge. Were it not for Anwar's encouragement and his colossal wealth, she would never have been able to afford a space so ample. She had always had to be careful with money, and now she could afford to paint as much as she liked, as large as she wanted, thanks to Anwar and his generosity.

What was their relationship? He was her patron, she decided. That's how she would reconcile that she was a kept woman. Whatever they had once felt for each other was in the past. She would paint her way to freedom, as Leonardo da Vinci had. Leonardo thought nothing of having the support of wealthy, powerful men. Without his rich patrons, he would have had nothing, Lucy reminded herself as she admired the day's work.

Prolific. That was the word that came to mind now that she had begun. Inspiration had possessed her. She hadn't confined herself to one style, suite of tools, or muse. She had unleashed everything she loved and knew.

Lucy glanced at the buckets of paint, mops, and giant sponges littering the floor. She didn't want to be dull or predictable. She wanted none of that. She had never belonged, so why start now? She was always the pink sheep surrounded by a pack of grey wolves.

Why try and paint what she thought people would want? She wanted, no, *she needed*, she corrected herself, *to paint what she felt*. What was the point of being an artist if all your paintings looked the same? She was a sea of cascading emotions, ever-changing like drifting sand across the desert.

More so now that she was pregnant with Anwar's child and the exhibition celebrating his birth was looming. Her emotions changed so rapidly she didn't know what she felt, but her paints did—flying across the bare canvas in cyclones of color. Whirls of carmine red collided with torrents of passion-infused pink, flooded in tumultuous crests of yummy yellows. Her paintings were like rainbow-coloured kaleido-scopes. Her paintings were landscapes from her heart.

Nothing she painted was half-hearted, she mused as her gaze swept over the artworks. She gave everything, just as she had given Anwar everything that fated night over eight months ago. But not again, she reminded herself. Now, she would only express the longings of her heart through her art. She feared getting attached. She knew that one day, she would find a way to leave before she surrendered to the impossible desert dreams that refused to die.

Love that lasted. A family that stayed together. Just the

three of them. Not a harem of wives and half-siblings. Not an uncertain future where people would stop at nothing to rule. She wanted to live in peace and bliss, not expose herself to unbearable pain. *Again.*

She'd rather live alone with her son and raise him as a single mother than endure her arranged marriage, whose only purpose was blind obedience to a man incapable of love.

She studied her hands. She was a compassionate finger-painter in the mud and tears of life, a co-creator of its sorrowful joy and beauty. She loved painting. She loved the freedom and thrill of it. She loved the way painting loved her back. Unconditionally, all-encompassing, enduringly.

And now she had a purpose. To fill the vast aircraft hangar with the deepest part of herself. To expose the pain she kept hidden, to paint the love she had not expressed. Her paintings would last forever, and her love would live on when she was gone. Perhaps then Anwar would realize what he had lost.

The best art is painted from a love of painting, she reminded herself. Not a preoccupation with self or pleasing others. She loved the rebelliousness of being creative. It was the one domain Anwar could not rule. She remembered growing up, being forced to shut her artistic tendencies down. She remembered the blatant disgust on his parent's faces, their ruthless impatience when she lingered too long to study something beautiful, their fortified disregard when she won prizes for her art, their constant put-downs and attempts to shame and blame her when she excelled.

What was wrong with them?

They hadn't understood her sensitivity to light, color, beauty—to pain. She grew hard or tried to, walling off her emotions, trying not to feel, to be like they were. She tried everything to be loved.

Only when she moved far away from her parents' hateful gaze did she start to paint and blossom. The first painting she created was of flowers. Big bright yellow flowers. A giant watercolor complemented with lime green leaves. It symbolized spring, hope, and new beginnings.

Her parents tried to steal her joy. And she had claimed it back. Now, she had been stolen by the sheikh. How ironic. A man who commanded that she paint with joy who couldn't, or wouldn't love her back.

She was unlovable. Not enough. Not worthy. Why else would her parents have treated her so? Why else would Anwar refuse to love her like a wife worthy of his adoration?

She was his possession. A surrogate of sorts, valuable only to bear his heir and help curate his collection for *Maerid al'ahlam: The Gallery of Dreams.*

And then what? What would become of her when the child was born, and the museum was open? Would he toss her aside like a used dishrag wife? Or would he surprise even himself and find room in his heart to love her? No, she was dreaming again.

She didn't know how or when she would escape with her son. She only knew she must.

CHAPTER TWENTY-FOUR

Anwar stood beside Lucy on the moonlit terrace, tall and commanding, exuding an aura of regality that seemed to permeate the air around him.

He looked so handsome, she mused as he was bathed in the soft glow of starlight. He had once told her he would never buy her flowers. She thought it was a strange thing to say. Now, surrounded by a natural aura of romance, she wished she had asked him why he felt that way. She sucked down a gulp of disappointment that he hadn't surprised her and gazed up at the stars. Heaven's flowers, she mused. Always in perpetual bloom.

"Every Valentine's Day, my friend Jane sends her daughters a box of chocolates," Lucy said, trying to break the palpable tension. "I used to think she was crazy for spoiling them that way. But now I realize she was showing them extra love. She was defying convention. I mean, who showers their kids with love on Valentine's Day?"

Jane's daughters were given more love than anyone could possibly understand. Why had she been so love-starved as a child? Lucy found herself wondering. Why was she being so malnourished now? She sighed. She would settle for a teaspoon of love, she reflected. No, *That's always been your problem. Settling,* she corrected.

"Valentine's Day is pure commercialism dreamt up by marketers to manipulate the masses," Anwar said. "The marketing executives probably sat in some stupid meeting and said, 'Sales are down. How can we spike demand? Wait, even better, how can we repeat it every year? We know—let's guilt trip, men.' Then they turned their attention to the lucrative female market and guilt-tripped mothers, only they're too easily manipulated to see. *Valentine's Day means nothing.*"

"Have you always been so cynical?" Lucy said.

"I'm a realist."

"And I'm a romantic," Lucy said. "I believe in love."

I just wish love believed in me.

"Do you believe in the tooth fairy too?" Anwar said.

"I used to."

"And then what?"

"Someone told me it was a lie."

"*Love is a lie,*" Anwar said. "Told in millions of ways— some small and some so big thousands of other lies are used as disguises.

"Says who?" Lucy challenged.

"Love destroys," Anwar lobbied with angry emphasis.

"Love saves. Love heals. *Love is love,*" Lucy threw at him. "Even if it's a made-up thing, I want to believe in it."

"Like Santa Claus?"

"Yes. Santa is reliable. He always shows up."

"Once a year? Is that all the love you want? From a man masquerading as a real person."

"No," she admitted. "I want more than that," Lucy said. "My friend Kate met her husband Gianni when he was—what was the word you used?" she paused for extra effect. "Oh, yes, when he was *masquerading* as Santa. She had survived the most horrific accident the Christmas prior and was plagued by survivor's guilt. Gianni Romano gave her the best gift ever. His everlasting love."

"You've got your present," Anwar said, gesturing to her pregnant belly. "You'll have that gift 24-7 for 20 years and more."

Lucy's face flamed with hurt.

"It worries me," he said. "*You worry me.*"

"I worry you?" she threw at him.

"The child will be a mommy's boy. He'll be spoiled rotten and never learn to be a man. And you, *habibti*, you will always have your cash cow. Giving birth to my heir will be the gift that keeps giving."

Lucy's hands flew to her hips. "Is that what you think?"

"What does it matter what I think?"

Lucy straightened, her mouth tight with fury. "You think I got pregnant to extort your wealth, right?"

Anwar's eyes darkened. "Didn't you?"

"You run hot and cold," she said resolutely. "No wonder I don't know where I stand with you."

There was silence as they stared into each other's eyes. She watched in almost complete detached fascination the angry quiver of his thick black lashes, the expansion of his pupils, the flame of anger.

She would meet anger with anger, she decided. No more compliant peacekeeping. No more righteous, silent anger. No more being accused of things she didn't do.

"I don't want anything from you," she exploded harshly. "I built my own career – at least, I did until you destroyed it. Not once, but twice," she said stonily. "I was doing well reinventing myself as an artist. Until you stole me and imprisoned me in your kingdom as your kept and reluctant bride," she added for good measure. "And I'm doing my best under excruciatingly trying circumstances to maintain my independence working as your curator and preparing for my exhibition. So don't you dare, *don't you bloody dare* accuse me of loving you for your money. I'm working my arse off."

"Loving me?" His eyes widened in surprise.

God, she'd said it—the bitter-sweet truth.

"Love is a lie," she said, wanting to retract her confession.

Anwar advanced toward her. "Says who?"

"Love destroys," she whispered, shrinking back.

"Says who?" His wide eyes watched Lucy with heated curiosity as he inched closer.

"Love destroys," Lucy stammered.

"Says who?" His breath fanned her heated face, smelling like Turkish Delight and honey.

"Love hurts like the worst kind of toothache. The only cure is to extract it from your life."

Anwar reached out to gently caress Lucy's cheek, his touch sending a shiver down her spine. The warmth of his hand against her skin felt like an electric current, igniting a fire within her. She leaned into his touch, her eyes closing momentarily, savoring the sensation. Their connection deepened as Lucy mirrored his gesture and intertwined her fingers with his. They stood there, locked in a silent embrace, their bodies yearning to be closer. Anwar's eyes held a mix of tenderness and desire. His gaze filled with an intensity that left Lucy breathless.

Slowly, Anwar leaned in, his lips hovering just inches away from Lucy's. Their breaths mingled, creating a sweet symphony of anticipation. Time seemed to stand still as they savored the moment, their hearts beating in unison.

And then, in a rush of emotion, their lips finally met. It was a gentle, tender kiss, soft and explorative as if they were discovering each other for the first time. Their mouths moved in perfect harmony, their kiss deepening, fueled by a passion that had been building for far too long.

Lucy felt her body melt into Anwar's, their embrace becoming tighter as if they were afraid to let go. The world around them faded away, leaving only the two of them lost in their own world of love and desire.

Their kiss spoke a language of longing, trust, and an unspoken promise of a future together. It was a kiss transcending time and space, a moment of pure bliss that would forever be etched in their hearts.

As they finally pulled away, their eyes met again, filled with a newfound connection Lucy felt in the depths of her heart. She felt so confused. It felt like it was just the beginning of a love story that would defy all odds, a love that would flourish and bloom as beautifully as the art Lucy created.

She gazed up at the stars, beseeching the heavens for a sign. She gave a tiny gasp as a star shot across the sky.

"Let's go to bed," Anwar murmured, taking her hand in his.

Was it too cliched, too impossible, and too good to be true? Had Anwar and Lucy found something extraordinary—a love that would last a lifetime, she wondered as she allowed herself to be led.

CHAPTER TWENTY-FIVE

"I love you," Anwar snuggled closer to Lucy, but instead of embracing him, she lay rigid as marble, her limbs stiffening like suffering *rigor mortis*. Her whole body felt stony, stiff, dead. Dead to his declaration of love. Dead to the risk he had taken sharing his heart. Dead to their dreams.

"What's wrong?" he asked, his voice fading like a deep, dying breath. *Why was this happening?*

She clenched her eyes and fisted her fingers.

"What's wrong?" Anwar asked again. *Was she trying to hurt him deliberately?*

"I can't," she gasped. "I can't do this."

"*This*?" he flew at her, jabbing his heart. "This," he said, pointing at her belly. "This– is that what you call us? A *this*? I love you, Lucy. Can you hear me? I love you. I thought it was what you wanted."

He hated the desperation in his voice. He hated who he was forcing himself to become. He hated that he couldn't, wouldn't, and didn't want to return to the person he once was. *He was a philandering playboy who never gave his heart*. He

had ceded his heart to her, allowed emotions to rule his intellect, and thrown caution to the wild winds. He wanted love, a
family, and her. He wanted it all.

"Lucy, speak to me."

Her hair fell across her face like a gold curtain as she
turned from him. She grasped at the sheets and wrapped the
silk around her like a cocoon. "I can't," she said. "I'm sorry."

"Are you deliberately tormenting me? Is this a game to
you?"

"Don't be cross with me," she whispered, refusing to
face him.

"Oh, right," he thundered. "Don't be cross. You've
scolded me for not sharing my feelings. Now, I share my
heart. But rather than reciprocate, you steal my soul. You tell
me you can't or won't commit." He raked his shaking hand
through his tousled hair.

"Anwar, please. I'm not ready—"

"Not ready for what? Not ready for a man who loves you
with all his heart? Not ready to start a family with a man in
love? Not ready for a life of happily-ever-afters, sunsets, and
sunrises?" He clutched at his chest. Suddenly, all the pain and
repressed memories of his past came tumbling back. "Is there
someone else?"

"Anwar!" She flung herself over and faced him. "No!
How can you even think that? There has only ever been you."

"I don't believe you." The force of his words startled him.
All he saw were broken hearts, free-falling from the sky and
shattering at his feet. "You have betrayed me. You have lied."

Emotion galloped ahead of him like fleeing Arabian stal-
lions racing against recapture. "Nobody's honest. Nobody's
true. *And now you*," he thundered. He felt like everything
good was gone. "I thought you felt differently. I thought our
love would save us from a world that's gone mad with narcis-

sistic self-obsession," he threw at her as he paced toward the door.

Anwar clenched his eyes shut as torrid memories began to rise. He needed to leave before he turned into his father. A violent despot who would kill rather than be left. A tyrannical husband who would destroy rather than be destroyed. A jealous tyrant who would—

No! He couldn't let those memories breathe. Anwar was not his father. He would never repeat his unthinkable sins. He turned to take one last look at the woman who had broken his heart. It was better that he left and never came back.

CHAPTER TWENTY-SIX

W hat have I done? Lucy pulled the bedsheets around her until she resembled an Egyptian mummy. Anwar was giving me everything I ever wanted. Why couldn't I take his heart when it was offered?

'Fear' came the answer. *Fear you're not worthy. Fear you'll be abandoned. Fear you're not loveable. Plain and simple.*

Why couldn't she shake her wounded past? Why did she keep sabotaging her happiness? It was so bloody irrational.

She ran her hand over the crumpled silhouette where Anwar had lain, pledging his love to her. The sheets had felt soft, sensual, and sexy as they cuddled together. But now they felt like sandpaper. Without him. Without his love. Without a future together. She had given him the cold shoulder and erased him from her life.

She shivered and pulled her hand away. The sheets upon which moments before Anwar and she had writhed in pleasure, kissing each other in the most intimate places, now felt cold. Without Anwar, she may as well be lying on an ice cube.

He wanted her in ways she didn't understand. For weeks, she had witnessed him wrestle with his emotions, his patience tested by their decision not to make love until their child was born. They had explored their bodies in every way possible. She had never wanted the night to end, and then, at last, he had repeated the words she had always longed to hear. His confession of love hadn't been a mirage. He had repeated the truth of his feelings over and over.

I love you. I love you. I love you.

And she had frozen. Frozen like the sheets now froze around her and her pregnant belly. She had lain frigid, dead to him, fearful of losing his love the moment it had been given.

She had to go to him before it was too late. She unwrapped herself from the tangled sheets and threw her feet out of the bed. She heard the unmistakable roar of Fazza's Lamborghini. His brother was helping him flee. The tires screeched on the pebbled forecourt as they accelerated. She ran to the window and cried helplessly as they sped away, fusing into the sunset as their love faded.

"*I love you, too*," Lucy shouted. "*Anwar, I love you.*"

But it was too late.

CHAPTER TWENTY-SEVEN

"I t's just too painful," Lucy confided to Issy Riley during her hastily arranged Zoom therapy call. "I feel —" she paused.

A long silence ensued. Lucy had experienced enough of Issy's counseling techniques to know she would wait for as long as it took for Lucy to process her emotions. She had taught her that silence was as therapeutic as talking. Sometimes, more so. If there were degrees in avoiding pain, Lucy would have a PhD, but she couldn't marinate her feelings in silence forever.

"I'm terrified," Lucy confessed at last. "I'm absolutely, bloody terrified."

"*Terrified*?" Issy reflected, the slight lilt of her voice inviting Lucy to expand her thoughts. It was less a question than an invitation to go deeper.

Lucy hesitated. Did she want to go deeper? If she told Issy her dreams, she risked everything. They would be diminished, no longer the fantasies of a traumatized teenager who dreamed of marrying a prince and living happily ever after. Instead, they would remain the mad visions of a woman who held them within her reach and fled when they were poised to become her living reality.

Lucy gulped as bitter realization flooded her awareness. "I'm sabotaging my happiness, aren't I?"

"*Are you*?" Issy asked.

"It's classic narcissistic abuse survivor syndrome," Lucy said.

"I don't believe in labels," Issy said. "Words can become things. Things you *don't* want. Like giant affirmations to the gods of misery."

"I can capture happiness in my paintings but can't make the feelings stick in reality," Lucy sobbed. "My love life is a disaster. And I am the wrecking ball," Lucy wept. "I'm sorry. I'm so sorry. I promised myself I wouldn't cry."

"Tears tell truths," Issy said softly.

"You have the patience of Mother Theresa. I wish Anwar did."

"Have you told him how you feel?"

"I can't."

"Can't or won't?"

Thundering finality drummed in Lucy's chest. "*He's gone.*"

"Gone?"

"He did a runner with his brother," Lucy said as sadness gave way to anger. "If he cared about me, he wouldn't have left me," she thundered, fury rising as all her fears of abandonment resurfaced. "It's so easy for him to make a run for freedom and leave me locked away in his wretched palace."

"You think Anwar should've stayed?"

"Of course he should've stayed! We're married."

"*Are you?* I thought you didn't want to marry him. Wasn't that what you told me?"

"Things are different."

"Different?"

"That was then."

"Then?"

"OK. It's true. I didn't love him when I signed the marriage contract. Not like I love him now. I love Anwar with all my heart. There, you made me say it. Are you happy now?" The words escaped before Lucy could censor them. "I'm sorry. That was a classic projection. My shadow got ahead of me."

Issy laughed. "You know you didn't need a session with me, Lucy. You have mastered everything I taught you. You could be a therapist."

"I just felt like talking to someone who really knows me. I don't have anyone," Lucy whispered.

"You have Anwar."

"I used to have Anwar."

"Open up to him. Tell him how you feel. Trust him with your heart."

"I don't know where he is. He's been gone for three days."

"And if you did? Would you be willing to share what you have told me?"

"That I love him?"

"Yes. That you love him with all your heart."

"Maybe," Lucy said.

"*Maybe?*"

"Okay. Yes."

Issy looked over her shoulder and pushed back from her chair.

"Lucy, can you hang on for a moment?"

"Sure. I'll nip out and get a glass of water."

Lucy heard muffled conversations in the distance as she

left her computer screen. She fetched a drink and sat back down at her desk.

"Anwar!"

"My bride," Anwar said, barely suppressing the faint smile that fluttered to his lips.

"You're in New Zealand?" Lucy exclaimed. "With Issy?"

"Yes, with Massimiliano and their children."

"Oh."

An awkward silence followed.

"Issy said you wanted to tell me something."

CHAPTER TWENTY-EIGHT

"My memories aren't good ones," Lucy said when Anwar returned to Avana several days later.

He stared at her, compassion in his eyes.

"All my life, the love I received was window dressing. A mirage in the desert. A family who smiled for the camera, disguising siblings at war, hatred for each other feeding on itself like a snake biting its tail."

A puzzled line crested his brows as he waited patiently for her to elaborate.

"Things carry an energetic footprint," Lucy continued. "Mediums and psychics can hold an object of a deceased person in their hands and channel them or at least communicate with them. I told the estate executor that I wanted nothing when my mother died. I wanted my family trauma to die with her. As far as I'm concerned, they are all dead."

"You're still angry," he said softly.

"No. Years of therapy have given me tools to release the anger I felt toward my childhood. But the wound is still there like a scar. Instead of a knife wound on my skin, it's in my heart. The lacerations of hurt and betrayal will never mend. I have to practice radical acceptance and make peace with my past."

"You make it sound easy," Anwar said.

"It is, and it isn't. The thing is, there is a simple truth that I now feel in my heart. *I'm done* living in the past." She turned to face Anwar. "I'd like to think the generational trauma ends with me. *With us.*"

Anwar suddenly saw the truth of what Lucy was saying. He suddenly felt the truth Lucy felt. He suddenly knew with definitive certainty there would be no happily ever after for their family as long as they lived in the past.

"Art has taught me again and again how to move on and begin anew. Sometimes, you've got to let everything go and purge yourself of the things, people, and circumstances weighing you down. Tina Turner once said, 'If you are unhappy with anything, whatever is bringing you down, get rid of it.' She said that's where we'll discover our freedom, our true creativity, our true self comes out."

"Tina Turner?"

"The singer."

"I know who she is."

"You look surprised," Lucy said.

"I didn't think—" Anwar began.

"Didn't think what? That a woman who survived the most horrific abuse by her husband, a woman who walked away with nothing but the name he gave her, a woman who was discriminated against for years, a woman, despite all the barriers she faced, became the world's most beloved entertainment star. You didn't think a woman like that could say something so profound?"

"I'm not the enemy, Lucy," Anwar said, raising his hands

in surrender. "Tina's absolutely right," Anwar spun around and pointed to the north. "We will begin again."

She followed his gaze through the bedroom window, traveling the length of the desert stretching before them like a blank canvas, full of possibility.

"After we have finished our other projects, I will build you a new home—a sandcastle of dreams. No matter how expensive the materials are, I want us to have a new future untainted by the past. Home," Anwar said. "What is that thing you Westerners say?"

"Home is where the heart is," Lucy said.

"What does this mean?"

Lucy shrugged. "I don't know. I've never felt it. Except, perhaps, here with you. For Arabs?" she asked, "What does home mean for you?"

"Home is rest," Anwar said, "A sacred place to restore amongst Divine Beings." He looked at her, ready for ridicule, but her wide smile encouraged him.

"That's so beautiful," she said. "I'd love to feel that. I've spent my whole life in chaos." She wrapped her arms around him and snuggled into his chest. "Tell me more about what home means for Arabs," she murmured.

"Being at one with nature," Anwar said. "Nature knows instinctively how to rest. We draw inspiration from Mother Earth and Father Sky. As above, so below. Sacred geometry connects them both. There is a time for rest and a time for work. A time for day, a time for night. Our homes directly link nature, home, and tranquillity."

"Is that why the palace has a courtyard and rooms open to the sky?"

Anwar nodded. "Our traditional ways of building are quickly being eroded." He gestured East to the city in the distance, "Western architecture has not only added the worst of Western life patterns— drinking, divorce, adultery, and crime—into our lives but also eroded its previous spiritual quality. Historical values have been forgotten. But with you, my love, with the family we will create, we can awaken lost dreams. We can take the best of both worlds—the innovations of Western technology and science and the spirituality of our ancestors. We can create a palace of profound healing and tranquillity where our souls can rest and replenish."

He folded his arms around her and lowered his face to the top of her head, kissing the silky blonde hair that shone like gold. "I would like to show you a surprise."

CHAPTER TWENTY-NINE

"What is this? Lucy said as Anwar took the silk blindfold from her eyes.

"Our son's bedroom."

Lucy's eyes widened as she scanned the walls lined with gleaming gold panels and the intricate marble floors polished to a high shine. "It looks like a bank vault."

"I want our son to feel treasured," he said. His lips curled downward as if his pride had been hurt.

"Like this?" Her head turned to face Anwar in a slow, disbelieving shake. "Do you want our son to feel like a toy boy living in a high-class jewelry box?"

Anwar's brow furrowed. "Everything is the best that money can purchase."

"Oh my god, what is this?" she thrust a finger toward the gold, bejeweled falcon perched fiercely at the crib's edge.

"I commissioned it from Massimiliano Balforni's atelier in Milan. He designed it personally."

"*He did*?"

"I told him what was important." Anwar pressed his hand to his chest and rubbed his hand over his heart.

"Which was?"

"That my son feels protected."

She pressed her palms to her cheeks. "*With that?*"

"The diamond and ruby-incrusted falcon is the only one in the world," Anwar said, reaching out to touch it.

"I bet!" Lucy said.

His dark brows knitted together. "You don't like it."

"You mean well. I know you do," she began. She loved Anwar too much to hurt him. "It's just, well... He looks so real... Those claws, that beak..." Her eyes rushed over the blood-red rubies gripped between the sculpture's claws. "He looks so menacing."

Anwar smiled. "Massimiliano has done a tremendous job of capturing the traits of a fierce protector. It's very realistic."

"The world is already too realistic," Lucy said softly. "I want our son to live in a world of dreams. The whole vibe needs softening."

"Softening!" Anwar spluttered.

Lucy's eyes drifted down to the black silk comforter in the crib, embroidered with Zephyr's face. "Do you think *that* will comfort our child?" she said, pointing to his fierce eyes, glinting with diamonds.

"The boy doesn't need comforting," he said. "He needs strength."

"This will give him nightmares." She sucked in a deep breath and turned to him. "Please don't be hurt," she said, registering his crestfallen face. "It's just—"

She hesitated. How to choose the right words? "*It's over the top.* There's no other way to say it."

"You can't give a child too much love," he said.

"This is where love lives." she pointed to Anwar's chest. "This is where the treasure is. Your heart is 24-carat gold. You can't buy love. Haven't you realized that yet?"

Anwar scowled.

Lucy gestured to a tiny, furry orange lion cub with chewed ears and flayed tuffs of hair. "What's this?"

"Simba," Anwar said.

"Simba?"

"Salim's toy."

"Oh," she whispered. She picked up the little lion and rubbed her finger over his golden fur. The soft velvet toy had been lovingly petted and tousled countless times by Salim as he healed from the trauma of the car accident. Her thoughts drifted to the tragic crash that had killed Anwar's older brother and his wife. Salim, clutching the toy to his heart, had survived the unsurvivable.

"It's adorable," she whispered, in awe of the miracle the toy had come to represent. Simba's expressive, dark chocolate eyes seemed to twinkle with mirth as if he held a secret treasure of happiness. Stitched with meticulous care, he wore an endearing smile that never faded, even after years of tender embraces.

"It's damaged," Anwar said, gesturing to the soft exterior that bore the marks of the accident. The scars were a testament to the ordeal he had endured. Yet, his spirit remained unyielding, just like the mighty lion he portrayed.

"I heard that Simba protected Salim, acting as a loyal guardian in the face of danger," Lucy said. "Along with your brother, who threw his body over Salim, Simba also bore the brunt of the shock. Before and after the accident."

"Yes," Anwar admitted. "It was Salim's comforter after —" he hesitated, not wanting to relive the fate that took his brother's life. "Salim has gifted Simba to our baby."

"Oh, that's so sweet," Lucy said. "Simba is so loved."

"I'm not sure it's a good idea. It's broken," Anwar said. "It's got bad memories."

"We all have bad memories. We're all broken." Lucy said. "That doesn't mean we should chuck everything out and replace it with shiny new things with no history. You think that is love. But it's not where the magic is." She thrust the soft toy towards Anwar's chest.

"Simba was Salim's cherished confidant, a friend who listened without judgment and offered solace with a gentle paw, wasn't he?"

Anwar nodded.

"I'm sure that they embarked on countless imaginative adventures together. Simba's presence would have been a constant source of comfort to the child," Lucy said.

Anwar clutched Simba in his hands, noticing for the first time the chewed ears his nephew had suckled. His heart lurched, remembering the painful day he had learned his oldest brother had been killed.

"I know it still hurts," Lucy said.

He stood silently, clutching the lion to his powerful chest.

"It's the first time I've seen you show emotion," she whispered.

Anwar heaved a deep breath, sucking painful memories deeper into his lungs.

"Let it out," she encouraged, wrapping her arms around him. "Let it go. Isn't that what you told me? To let the grief escape."

Anwar drew her to his side. She leaned into his powerful chest, feeling it thump as she did so.

"*Marhabaan, habibti*. Hello, my love," he whispered.

"What is soft is strong," she said as his body slumped against hers. Lucy laced her fingers through Anwar's dark mane of hair. "Lions are strong, lions are courageous, lions are powerful. Lions are also loyal—they feel everything deeply—even grief. Especially grief," she emphasized.

Anwar drew a gulp of air and exhaled, the tension escaping from his chest as his shuddering breath grew quieter.

"This little lion is a symbol of courage, of resilience. Of new life—despite the pain of our pasts," Lucy said.

"You are right, *habibti*. Salim is a young man, and he has cherished his faithful companion for years. Simba's well-loved presence reminds us that even the soft can possess an indomitable spirit. This little lion offers a testament to the enduring power of love, bringing joy and comfort to all who cross his path."

Anwar pulled the comforter from the crib and draped it over the jeweled falcon. "Very well. Simba will be our son's protector," he said as he lay the little lion in the crib.

"What is soft is strong," Lucy repeated.

"We will find somewhere else for this magnificent sculpture," Anwar said, resting a hand on the fierce jewel-crusted falcon.

"Love creates love. Love is love. Love feels like this," she said, drawing him to her chest. Her eyes fell upon a magenta and violet orchid in a gold urn. She walked toward it and lowered her head. 'It smells divine. I love it. Where did you buy it?"

A wide smile spread across his face. "I grew it."

"*You did*?" she said disbelievingly.

"Wow. I'm impressed. It's so beautiful," she turned to him. "You poured your heart into it, didn't you."

"Yes."

"I tried to grow orchids once. It's not easy. What's your secret?"

"I talk to them. I tell them how special they are. I touch them. . ."

"You shower them with love and affection."

"Yes," he said, awareness dawning.

"Children are like flowers," Lucy said. "They don't grow in gold-lined tombs studded with diamonds. They thrive on tenderness, kindness, and kisses. Children love caressing touches and whispers from your heart. That is how you show your love."

"Ok. You win," Anwar laughed. "Point taken. Second-hand toys and flowers are how I show my love."

"And this is how I show you love." Lucy lifted her face to his and placed a kiss on his lips.

"There's just one more thing," she murmured.

CHAPTER THIRTY

Stay in your heart, Lucy affirmed to herself as she prepared to tell Anwar how she would like to raise their child.

"I want my son to be raised by the stars."

"What are you talking about?" Anwar said.

"By the sun and the planets," she said, gazing at the full moon. A full moon in Leo. The courageous moon. "We will raise him by astrology."

"We will raise him as I was brought up," Anwar said.

"Yes, and look how that worked out," Lucy said. "Your father deprived you of love and affection because he wanted you to be fierce and unfeeling. Instead, he made you feel unloved and unwanted. I want our child to know what true love is. I want to raise our son to be true to himself."

"That is a luxury reserved for Westerners and fools," Anwar said. "My son's role will be duty, as mine was."

"Our son will be born to rule as you were. Loving him won't change that. We need him to be a good ruler. A kind ruler. A benevolent ruler. A ruler with so much confidence and self-esteem that the thought of being cruel has no place in his heart. To do that, we need to break the cycle."

"What cycle?"

"The generational trauma."

"And just how do we do that?"

"I told you. Astrology. Or rather parentology," Lucy corrected. She fixed him with a gaze that said without words, 'Don't betray me.'

"We both agreed we need to put our child first." She waited until Anwar gave an almost imperceptible nod. "Your parents believed in raising you in a strict environment. It wasn't right for your personality. Parenting is tricky but doesn't have to be a guessing game. By knowing a little about our offspring's classic characteristics, we can gain insight into what drives him. We can get a head start and give him one too. We can learn how to make things easier and help him to thrive."

He looked at her and rolled his eyes. "Depending on his horoscope?" Anwar brushed some lint from his jacket. "Next, you'll tell me to put my faith in tea leaves," he said tonelessly.

"You can relax," Lucy said, ignoring him. "Your Libran child will be a neat freak like you. So don't stress. There won't be many toys left lying around to spike your perfectionist streak."

"I know. I have servants for that."

"And Librans are peacekeepers—this bodes well for his role of maintaining harmony in the kingdom. And the Libran child loves to be social. He will welcome people to the Kingdom and help keep Avana on the world stage. But we must put extra caution around him—lest he gets steered toward unsavory strangers. Because the Libran child is trusting."

Anwar's arms crossed over his chest, restrained strength pouring through them. "*So he will be naive.* That worries me."

"Your Libran son will see the best in people. Looking for what's wrong in others only amplifies the worst. You should know the danger of that better than anyone," she said. "Every time someone sees an Arab board a plane, they think they're a terrorist. Anyway, your guards will protect him," Lucy said. "Besides, the Libran child is loved by one and all. He'll be balanced. Sociable. And kind. *Genuinely kind.* Not pathologically, narcissistically, manipulatively kind," she added. "Making friends will never be an issue for our child."

"What did you mean when you said my parents didn't raise me according to my personality," Anwar asked.

"You're a Taurus. What can I say?" she shrugged, splaying her hands wide.

"Enlighten me," he said fiercely.

"You're strong, independent and *wilful.* But you are also soft-natured and loving. Taurean children love to snuggle up to their parents for warmth and a secure feeling. You didn't get any of that growing up. Imagine if you had, you wouldn't be carrying around all that generational trauma. You might've been more creative if your parents had raised you according to your astrological sign. *You might have been an artist!* Instead, your obsessive need to always be in control and determination for things to go how you desire has made you stubborn."

"I am not," Anwar said, stomping his foot.

"Prove it," Lucy said calmly. "Let me raise our Libran son by the stars."

Anwar frowned. His stern gaze fixed on Lucy's beautiful face. "My son is a warrior, not a girl."

"See what I mean," she said, sighing heavily. "You won't

even try. *That's so Cold War*. Look at the planet. All this warmongering. Where has it got us?"

His dark brows furrowed into a troubled line."Nowhere."

"Thousands of sons and daughters, strewn over battle-fields, killed in wars they never wanted. Millions of people forced from their homes. A life of terror—is that what you want for your son? Worrying about whether your neighboring rulers will mount an invasion."

"Of course not." He looked skyward as the first stars trembled into life in the indigo sky.

She felt the torch she carried inside her flame like a fire. "The Dalai Lama once said that we need more artists and healers on the planet."

"The Dalai Lama lost control of his country," Anwar said.

He argued about everything Lucy told herself. But in the matter of raising their son, she would not be defeated.

"The Dalai Lama's prayers were no match for the Chinese Military's armed invasion of Tibet. The fight was never fair. His country was stolen from him," Lucy said. "Our son's creativity, if nurtured, could lead to great innovation, and his gift for diplomacy could lead to a different way to ensure peace."

"*Could*."

"Would."

"And you, Lucy? What of you? How will you help ensure the peace and prosperity of the kingdom your son will one day rule?"

"Art is the highest form of hope," she said.

"*Hope*," Anwar said sardonically.

"Why are you being so belligerent? We are creating more hope in the region by building *Maerid al'ahlam: The Gallery of Dreams*. Have you ever noticed that anytime there's a war, even when the Nazis stormed through

Italy, the orders were clear, '*No one is to destroy the artistic treasures.*'

"Hitler was a complex character," Anwar said.

"We're all complex," Lucy agreed.

"Things are different now. Invaders seek to destroy culture. They burn the books, destroy the sculptures, desecrate all that is beautiful."

"You always said the dark forces can not steal the light. You know as well as I that we can all be healed by art. Art can break down stereotypes, whether a painting, a sculpture, a building, or the lines in a song or story. Art can pull down the barriers of mistrust between warring communities and pave the way for reconciliation and justice. So to answer your question, what I will do, no what we will do," she corrected, "is continue to create an artistic legacy devoted to enduring peace and prosperity."

Anwar regarded her skeptically.

"Why are you being so obstinate," she threw at him. "You know I'm right. Look at what your brother Tariq and Melanie achieved with their museum, HABI. Melanie's innovative, world-first design won the coveted architecture award, the Ritzher. Not only was she the first architect to win, but she cemented his vision for his museum—a fun and educational place to house all the activities related to his animal conservation projects. People, tourists, scientists, conservationists, media—a wide and diverse group of people, now come under one roof, united by a common cause to protect endangered animals and save the planet."

She sensed his conviction had wavered, his self-belief impacted by the scar of his father's inability to love him and his constant criticism. His vulnerability in that moment made her love him more.

"Our project will do the same—attract tourists and diversify our income away from relying on fossil fuels, " she reinforced. "You said it yourself: it will boost the economy and enrich the lives of your people," she said, forcibly affirming his vision.

A man must be strong enough for you to respect him but weak enough for you to love him, she thought to herself as she saw the strength in his vision return under the fierce force of her belief in him.

"Have I ever told you how much I admire you," he said, lowering his face to hers and kissing her. "You are fierce like a lion and tender like a star. *Ahwa.* I am in love."

"*Ahwa, habibti,*" she murmured as his tongue danced with hers. "I also am in love." And this time, instead of words mingling with anticipation and fear, she tasted honey.

She placed a hand on her swollen belly. "Let's take our son for one last visit to where it all began."

CHAPTER THIRTY-ONE

L ast night had been about intimacy. About giving each other joy. It had been about forgiving the past and celebrating the new life that awaited, Lucy thought, slipping from the sheets and standing outside the tent.

They had journeyed to the building site where the Gallery of Dreams would be built and decided impulsively to stay the night. It had been a perfect evening in every way. It was exciting to see the earthworks beginning and the site being prepared for the construction planned for the New Year. Once all the workers had gone home, they were alone in their royal tent with their love, their dreams, and the stars.

The sandstorm approached so gracefully that, at first, Lucy didn't register the threat. She had been on such a euphoric high, and she wanted to enjoy the peace and beauty of the desert with the man she loved.

She glanced at the horizon as the cloud of dust grew thicker. Should she be worried, she wondered? It spiraled with increasing urgency, like some ominous dance, covering everything in a dusty haze until everything in the distance was buried.

Were it not so menacing, it would be beautiful, Lucy thought, momentarily beguiled. Billowing clouds of sand, infused with champagne golds and rose pinks and edged with creamy white, set perfectly against a moody night sky. Suddenly, searing pain jolted her senses awake.

"Anwar! Anwar!" she cried, her tone raw with urgency. She shuddered and clenched her fingers around his stomach as he drew to her.

"Get inside," he commanded as a large whooshing roar filled the air.

"The baby—" she winced as contractions pummelled through her. "No! He can't come now. Not here. Not like this," Lucy screamed, clenching the sheets as Anwar picked her up and lay her on the bed.

"I want to go to the hospital. I want my baby to have the best care."

"And you think I don't? Do you think I want my child born in a tent like a commoner?"

If it weren't for the pain ripping through her, Lucy would have commented on the grandeur of the tent, the luxury, the wealth. Their son was hardly entering the world like a pauper.

She suppressed a scream as a painful contraction lashed through her groin. Sand pummelled the tent, raining its unrelenting fury.

"Why?" She hurled at the storm, "Why can't it be easy?"

"Strength, my love," Anwar said, his voice softening as he held her hand, "What is soft is strong. Relax."

She smiled at him, suddenly feeling safe and protected. Where other women may have cursed and sworn at their partners as pain overtook them, Anwar was echoing the advice of the midwife who had tended to her since her arrival. Instinctively, her body wanted to tense, but she bent all her willpower to do as Anwar encouraged and relaxed.

"I will get you through this," he assured her as she exhaled painful wooshes of breath in rapid succession. "Tell me what to do," he said, wiping the beads of sweat from her brow.

"I don't know," Lucy said, clenching as another contraction riveted through her belly. "In the movies—" she began, "Boiling water. To sanitize."

"In the old days before ambulances and hospitals, all women, princesses, and queens," Anwar said, rising to his feet and kissing her forehead. "They all had their babies in the desert. Like you—"

"Jesus!" she cursed.

"Yes, your Jesus, king of kings, was born in a dusty manger on a bed of hay."

"I don't want to have a baby in the sand," she grimaced. "What if something goes wrong?"

"Nothing will go wrong. The stars are aligned. Venus is appearing like an angel in the sky, spreading her wings." he clapped his hands. "Our baby will soon be born. Look, Lucy. Just like your nativity story. Following a great big star. Three kings were riding on their camels through the dusty desert, with a star to guide the way."

"A star won't deliver my baby," she cried. "Will anyone come? A nurse? A doctor? You must have someone." She gripped his hand as shards of pain shot through her. The roar of the wind drowned out her muffled cries.

"Let go," Anwar commanded as she clamped her mouth. "Scream! Don't keep your feelings inside."

"No!" she cried, writhing as a contraction jolted through her.

"There is no shame in expressing pain," he reassured her.

"In our culture, women wail, they cry, they bellow. You are giving life to life. Roar. Shout. Scream—do anything other than be quiet."

"In my culture," she threw at him, "Women who cry are weak!" She gritted her teeth and looked beyond his concerned face. Through the tent's flapping opening, she could see a solitary palm. Its trunk stood firm and stoic like an iron rod, but the leaves flailed and heaved in despair and fury, fighting against the storm.

"No!" she screamed.

"Louder!" He commanded. He ripped the fine cotton of his *dishdashi* into strips and plunged it into the pot of boiling water over the small fire in the center of the tent. He fished it out with iron tongs, waited for it to cool slightly, and then wiped her brow with it.

"My son will be strong like his mother. Yet sensitive to pain," he said. "He will not be a tyrant, a despot, a man impervious to the suffering of his people."

She writhed and clenched the sheets. "I think he's coming. Oh my God, I think he's coming!"

"Push!" Anwar cried.

"Go!" she screamed. She didn't want Anwar to see her with a baby's head about to push through the place he considered sacred. "No man wants to see this."

"But I do," he said, kneeling before her, his hands splayed, ready to take his son in his arms.

The wind whistled like a kettle. The sand flew past the tent in horizontal sheets.

"Push!" he urged. "I can see his head!"

Lucy summoned the last of her ebbing strength.

"Again!"

"I can't," Lucy said.

"You can!"

She clenched her teeth, sucked in a deep breath and pushed.

"Once more. I see him. I see our prince."

"*Marhabaan, habibti.* Hello, my love," He whispered as his hand gently held the baby's head. "He's beautiful like an angel. Push, my love. Push. Push like a lioness would. Wild and strong, fierce with her love."

The storm rose in fury as though helping her deliver her baby that would one day rule the desert. The child slipped from her womb like a fast-moving river in flood. Anwar cut and tied off the umbilical cord, joining mother and child with a deft slice from his royal saber. The baby lay in Anwar's arms, cooing and gurgling like popping champagne.

"*Habibti. Habibti.* My love. My love–" he said, his eyes flaring wide.

"What is it? What's wrong with my baby?"

"*Habibti. Habibti.* My love, my love," he repeated.

"What's wrong? Tell me."

"Nothing is wrong."

"You're keeping something from me."

"It's a miracle, my love. A miracle."

"What? Please tell me. What?"

"Our baby. . . our baby. . . our baby…"

"What is it?"

"*She's a girl!*"

CHAPTER THIRTY-TWO

Habibti "Rabah Minnie na Hassir," Anwar affirmed. "A very fine name for a very fine young lady."

"You were the scapegoat because you allowed it," Anwar had said to her once. His words echoed through her mind as she watched the Bedouin goats gnawing on desert shrubs beyond the palace walls.

She wasn't going to remain mute and be the scapegoat anymore, she vowed, fisting her fingers. It wasn't right. It wasn't honest. It wasn't the truth. Some things couldn't remain buried.

Later that evening, while their daughter slept blissfully in her nursery, Simba, tucked beside her, she went in search of Anwar. It was time to test the strength of Anwar's love for her.

"Hamad is still blaming me for *his* decisions," she said, entering his study. "Hamad was the one who had trusted the art broker and bought Salvator Mundi at auction. I told him it was an over-priced, highly questionable painting. The painting's provenance was too perfect, too carefully curated, just as the painting's restoration had been. After the restorer's work, I doubt any of Leonardo's brushstrokes were left. I don't know why Hamad was so determined to possess it. Salvator Mundi, Saviour of the World, isn't even Islamic. Leonardo had painted the face of Christ. A Christian god of sorts," Lucy said. "But Jesus wasn't even a god. He was a mortal, just like you and I," she conceded. "Like our child, born on a dusty manger. But here's the other thing. Our child isn't going to wear the shame of the stain against my reputation."

"You have been absolved," Anwar reminded her, placing his pen down and regarding her intently.

"Yes, in a British court. But Western absolution still carries an admission of guilt in your people's world. I am being forced to remain silent and take the blame so your brother can keep his honor. What about my honor? Or don't I merit your protection?"

"I know you're innocent."

"You're the only one. *In everyone else's eyes, I'm guilty.* It's not right. I won't allow it."

"What would you have me do? Revolt against my family?"

"I did."

"It's different."

"Why?"

"Your culture values individuality. My people are tribal. Clans are important. The collective must always prevail."

"I am your collective," Lucy threw at him. "We are your collective. Our daughter, you, and I, we are family. We are your clan," she said, gesturing to the life-size photographic portrait of the three of them, spotlighted on the feature wall behind his desk. "You once told me that honesty and loyalty were your treasures above all else. You told me that trust had to be earned. You've got a weird way of showing it, Anwar. Does it only go one way?"

"I have given you my heart."

"I want more."

"More?" he said incredulously.

"I want you to give me your word. I want you to tell everyone what Hamad has done."

She slept alone that night, too restless and angry to pretend it didn't matter. A montage of memories played through her mind. She thought of the times she'd been scapegoated and blamed for her sibling's greed when her mother died. Guilt-shamed with demands of toxic platitudes of gratitude. 'You should be happy that mom left you anything at all.' She was grateful; of course, she was. But the truth was she had received a third of what they inherited. Her sister had coerced and manipulated her mother to change her will as she lay on her deathbed. God only knows what lies she fabricated to get her mother to agree.

They lied, concealed, and stole from her and then had the audacity to tell her that she should be grateful. Lucy still blamed herself. She had been blind. Always placating, always conceding, always pleasing, and putting herself last.

'You could have fought back. You should have taken them to court. You would've won,' her friends had censored. *Would, could, and should*—the three ugly brothers, hurling recrimination and shame.

Could have what? Could have spoken up? Should I have challenged their behavior? Would there have been a better ending? Hadn't Anwar said the same thing? "You should be grateful Hamad has agreed not to take legal action. You would do well to count your blessings."

Did Anwar really believe she should be thankful that Hamad wasn't prosecuting her now via some archaic Arabic justice process to atone for his mistakes?

"You should just let it go," Anwar had said.

Let it go.

She hated that the most. Turn a blind eye to injustices and look the other way. No, she'd done it before, and where it had got her? It was time she fought back and stood up for herself. If not for her, for her daughter.

"I'm sick of being the scapegoat for other people's crimes," she told Anwar the following morning over breakfast.

Anwar grinned. "You do not look like a goat."

"It's not funny, Anwar."

"Ok. What is this scapegoat that has hurt you so much?"

"Everyone loads their shit on the goat's back so they can unburden themselves of their lack. Lack of honesty. Lack of loyalty. Lack of kindness, love, compassion..." the words came tumbling out in a river of anger and pain.

"Why a goat? A donkey or camel can carry more. They are stronger," he said, reaching out for her hand playfully. "You are stronger."

She pulled away from him. Too hurt and too furious that he was not taking her seriously. "People who scapegoat you don't want you to be strong. They want to weaken and sacrifice you."

Anwar gestured to the servants to pour Lucy a strong cup of traditional Arabic coffee and passed her a plate of dates. "To sweeten the morning!" he murmured.

But Lucy was in no mood to be placated. "In the Bible, a

goat was sent into the wilderness after the priest symbolically laid the people's sins upon it. The goat's throat was slit."

"Lucy, I have given you my word. Nothing will happen to you."

"But it has happened."

"This isn't just about Hamad, is it?" he said, awareness washing over his face in empathetic understanding.

"No," she whispered, staring into the steaming black abyss of the coffee. Why couldn't she let go of the darkness that stained her heart? Why couldn't she be happy with what she had? Why couldn't she reflect upon her blessings, which she had many, instead of her misfortunes? She shook her head. "I'm trying to let go, Anwar. Really I am. It's the injustice."

"I know," he said softly, watching her with patient silence as she picked at the dates.

"Few things are harder to bear than being scapegoated by your family. Blamed for the wrongdoings, mistakes, and faults of others. Assaulted by hostility by those who are meant to show you love. Instead, the scapegoat is symbolically slaughtered so the community can atone for their sins."

His brow furrowed. "Please help me understand."

"Let me give you an example. A woman who has fought with her boyfriend may kick her dog for minor misbehavior when she comes home. The dog becomes the scapegoat and pays the price for her earlier fight with her boyfriend."

"Kicks her dog! That's abuse."

"How about this for an appalling example? It's fictional, of course. To protect his family's honor, a rich, self-entitled fool who realizes he's been defrauded in a sophisticated art scandal, instead of taking responsibility for not listening to warnings from the family's trusted art advisor, blames her for his mistake. She becomes the scapegoat. She's expected to allow him to escape from his stupidity, remain blameless, and avoid paying the price. The fool feels better about himself and slaughters the innocent art advisor's reputation and career. Then they gaslight her and tell her there's nothing to worry about. She should just let go, forget about it. Leave it in the past."

"*Gaslight*?"

"Honestly, Anwar," Lucy said, rolling her eyes. "Gaslighting is a form of psychological manipulation where someone deliberately tries to make another person doubt their perception, memory, or sanity. The gaslighter uses tactics such as denying facts, twisting the truth, manipulating situations, and questioning the victim's reality, making them feel confused, insecure, and self-doubting. The goal of gaslighting is to gain power and control over the victim by making them question their judgment and rely on the gaslighter's version of events. It is a harmful and manipulative behavior that can have significant emotional and psychological effects on the victim."

"And who is the victim?"

"*I am the victim.* I will always be the victim as long as Hamad gets away with what he did. Whether I like it or not. Something, or someone, has to change—and it's not me!"

CHAPTER THIRTY-THREE

That evening, Hamad entered Lucy's studio nervously, clutching a bouquet of orchids.

"Hamad!"

Hamad sucked a deep breath. "Lucy, I owe you an apology. A sincere and humble apology."

"*Has Anwar spoken to you*?" she asked regarding him warily.

Hamad shook his head. "No, why?"

"Nothing." Her brows crested as she tried to work out the puzzle of why Hamad had entered the confessional of her studio after all this time.

"It's about the accusation I made against you, accusing you of art fraud. I want you to know that it was all a lie, a fabrication born from my jealousy and insecurity."

Lucy's mouth gaped open. "*Jealousy? Insecurity?* I don't understand."

Hamad lowered his eyes and studied the maze of rainbow-colored blobs of paint splattered on the studio floor. "Lucy, I have watched you and Anwar since you first met. The love and joy you found in each other's company was evident and consumed me with envy. I wanted what Anwar had, and I couldn't find it. Believe me, I tried," he gave a feeble laugh, then drew his body erect and looked into her eyes.

Where normally Hamad looked haughty and arrogant, she now saw vulnerability and remorse. What had come over him to make such a dramatic change? By speaking aloud, her intention that she would no longer be scapegoated, had she awoken some inexplicable change? She warned herself to stay alert to manipulation. How could she be sure of his true motive? He'd lied over and over and over—why not again?

"I couldn't bear to see the bond you both shared, and it clouded my judgment."

Her breath caught in her throat. This was not the confession she had expected. "You mean to say that you accused me of art fraud because of your jealousy towards Anwar? You caused me all that hurt and pain *because you were envious.*"

"Yes, Lucy, that's the shameful truth. I was afraid of losing Anwar's love and affection. I convinced myself that by tarnishing your reputation, I could somehow protect what was mine."

Wow, she thought. Just wow. Hamad was pouring his heart out to her, and deep in her gut, she knew his remorse was genuine.

"I have come to realize the immense damage I have caused, not only to you but to our entire family as well."

Tears welled in Lucy's eyes as the hurt and hardship his actions had caused rose in her consciousness. "You caused me such heartbreak, Hamad," she whispered. "But why are you confessing? Why now?"

"I've met someone," he mumbled.

"*You've met someone*! And that's why you want my forgiveness?" Had she been too quick to default to her old ways and believe the best in others? Was it his selfish agenda that now caused him to confess?

"I know what you're thinking, Lucy. And you're right. But you're also wrong. *I am being selfish.* But I hope you'll understand it is a good kind of selfishness. I don't want to keep on being Hamad the Horrid. I deeply regret my actions. I know I can't undo the pain I have caused you, but I hope you can find it in your heart to forgive me. I am truly sorry for betraying your trust and tarnishing your name."

"*Because you've met someone,*" Lucy repeated firmly. All she could see was red. Flaming, fiery, furious red. She wanted to rain her unexpressed rage against him for the damage he had done in a fireball of righteous anger.

She forced her heart to slow, took deep, measured breaths, and counted to ten. What sort of a role model would she be as a mother, a wife, and a leader with Anwar of their kingdom if she couldn't find it in her heart to forgive?

What color is forgiveness, she wondered, as her gaze fell upon the bouquet of scented orchids. *White. The color of peace.*

"I am a deeply flawed person," he mumbled. "But I want to be a better man. I want to change. Can you help me? Can you forgive me?"

He plucked the white orchid and handed it to her, then pressed the bouquet toward her to symbolize his sincerity.

"Our father," he began, "I know it's not an excuse, but he taught us to fight against each other. At least as far as I was concerned. He was always pitting me against my brothers. I envied their closeness. Oh, how I wanted that closeness with them. But my father wouldn't allow it. I don't want to go into the detail, I'll spare you that, but," he paused, gulping great gasps of air as the lived trauma flooded back. "The torture—"

Lucy held her palm in the air. "It's okay, Hamad. I know

something of your father's legacy. You don't need to speak of the unspeakable. At least not with me. I know a good counselor if you would consider talking to her. Issy helped me."

Lucy looked at the flowers and then up at Hamad, contemplating his pain and words. After a moment of contemplative reflection, she took a deep breath.

"Forgiveness is a difficult thing, Hamad. But I believe in the power of healing and second chances. While what you did was hurtful, I see the remorse in your eyes. I understand the pain your father inflicted on you. I know how hurtful it is when those who are supposed to want the best for you only see glory in your demise. And I can sense your genuine desire for redemption."

She placed the flowers on the table by her easel and sat beside him. "I forgive you, Hamad. I'd be glad to put the whole thing behind us. I hope you mean it when you say you will strive to be a better person. It's hateful and hurtful to tell lies." She reached out and clasped his trembling hands in hers.

Hamad tried to speak, but no words came out. Tears welled in his eyes. Finally, after a lengthy silence, he spoke. "Thank you, Lucy. Your forgiveness means more to me than words can express. I promise I will do everything I can to make amends and regain your trust. You deserve nothing less."

They both sat silently for a moment, the weight of the conversation hanging in the air. They both shared a hopeful smile, knowing that forgiveness was the first step toward reconciliation and healing.

"Here," Lucy said, getting to her feet and walking to her paints. She plunged a giant mop into a bucket of white paint. "Let's move forward from this dark chapter," she said, passing the mop to him. "Let's paint a new story and focus on recreating what was lost and giving life to what will be."

He looked at her uncertainly. "I'm not an artist. I don't know how to paint."

"Like this," she said, her eyes shining as she locked her gaze on a giant canvas."

She plunged another mop in a bucket of paint and thrust it forward. "Forgiveness feels fabulous," she cried as the paint landed with a smack.

Hamad's slumping posture straightened in shock. He covered his mouth with his hand, then rose to his feet. He uttered a soft prayer and then cried out in release. "Lucy is merciful," and swept the painted loaded mop in sweeping rhythmic hearts.

Hamad had changed, and Lucy found she had, too. Facing their painful pasts had led to growth for everyone.

Lucy reached for a giant crayon and scrawled, "With time and effort and love, healing is possible."

CHAPTER THIRTY-FOUR

The exhibition was looming, and Lucy was in no way ready. Ideas were still swirling around, diffusing and dissipating, but now it was time to finish a coherent body of work. She studied the blank canvases looming large along the walls and sucked in a deep breath.

Just do it! Don't overthink it!

She plunged the floppy mop into the bucket of diluted magenta paint. Magenta is the color of universal harmony and emotional balance, she reflected. Magenta contains red's passion, power, and energy—restrained by violet's introspection and quiet energy. Magenta promotes compassion, kindness, and cooperation. Magenta was the color of cheerfulness, happiness, contentment, and appreciation.

Magenta embodies unconditional love.

Would Anwar love the collection? While she wasn't seeking Anwar's approval, Lucy hoped he would love what she created. She was celebrating their love and the winding journey their hearts had traveled. And she was celebrating the birth of their daughter. It suddenly made sense now why, all those times she had tried to paint blues, she didn't feel it. Her baby was a girl, not a boy like the sonographer had told her during her mid-pregnancy ultrasound in New York.

"Be fearless," she encouraged herself. "Be brave. Fortune favors the strong." Wrenching the mop from the bucket, dripping with shimmering pigment, she lunged at the canvas, exhaling noisily from deep in her belly.

"Love!" she shouted. "Lock onto love!"

She swept the mop vigorously along the canvas, then repeated similar movements with each of the 12 canvases lined across the walls of her studio. Her arms tingled with pulsing conviction as her confidence grew bolder with each flourish.

"Love rules. Love matters. Love is the real world."

Love was no longer a dream. No longer an unanswered prayer. It was no longer abstract but tangible and real because of Anwar and Minnie. Lucy worked quickly, saturating the canvas with her inspired emotions. She felt free. Happy. In her element. The giant canvases confronted all the small fragmented aspects of her past she no longer wished to carry. Her childhood may have been stolen, but the precious riches buried deep in her soul lived.

Without her wounds, what would she have to paint? she laughed.

She stepped back and viewed the paintings from a distance. What do they need?

Contrast.

"A good painting is a mix of sameness and contrast. Opposites attract in life and art," Lucy said, taking a soft-bristled paintbrush. She layered in subtle strokes of inky-navy within the vibrant jolts of magenta pink. Anwar was navy to her and her daughter's magenta. Strong. Reliable. Safe. His love had brought stability to their lives. His love had birthed her dreams into reality.

Brush in hand, launching between canvases, Lucy was in her body. She was working with her mind rather than against it. She was in her heart rather than detached from it. She was engaged, present, and receptive.

She stood back and saw the idea's potential unfolding in a kaleidoscope of intuitive, divinely guided inspiration. She worked rapidly, dancing as she painted.

At last, she was done. Trembling and excited, she knew not to overwork the paintings. They pulsated with life. They held gesture, emotion, and meaning. She had begun with a blank canvas and made something exhilarating.

Her hand trembled slightly as she added a bold signature. What to call it, she wondered. *Healing is Possible,* came the answer as she placed her brush down.

The only question remaining unanswered is how her latest works would be received. What reception would they, *she*, receive when they were unveiled? Their reaction was beyond her control. Anwar and his wealthy collector friends would either love them or detest them.

CHAPTER THIRTY-FIVE

The day had finally come—the unveiling of her latest works. But first to paint the canvas of her face. But what look to curate? Understated elegance, she decided.

"Let the paintings shine, not me," she whispered as she dabbed a little lush tint called *Ascend* on her cheeks and patted her skin with her fingertips to create a glow from within. She added a touch of *Radiance Moon* to the same area to create a dewy sheen. She then applied eye pigment in a soft nude shade with a flat brush and blended it with her fingertips. She used Radiant Sun through to the center of her lid along the outer corner of the eye and repeated the process with her other eye.

She curled her lashes and added mascara, then added a whisper of styling wax to create a soft, no-fuss, brushed-up feel to her brows. Lastly, she swept matt lipstick in her favorite nude hue so she didn't look overdone. The last thing she wanted was for Anwar to think she was trying to outclass the collection he had commissioned. She studied her reflection in the mirror. Her stomach gurgled in disapproval. "I've taken the understated look too far, haven't I?" she said to her reflection. "Instead of subtle knockout, I just look plain."

It was time to go big or go home, she decided. Hadn't she done that with her paintings? She'd spent her life dimming her light, heeding her mother's call not to outshine others. She needed to go bolder. "Out with Plain Jane and in with Magic Marilyn," she affirmed, referencing one of her muses, Marilyn Monroe.

"What would Marilyn do?" she asked.

She would embrace the sultry summer desert vibe and go for glowing skin, pops of bright colors, and even a touch of glitter.

"Be glamorous," Marilyn encouraged as Lucy amped the shimmer and shine.

She would hit the opening party for the exhibition, ready to toast her huge accomplishment and dance the night away.

She picked out her outfit and put on a party playlist to set the mood. As Tina Turner belted out her heroic tune *The Best*, Lucy illuminated the high points of her cheeks, shimmering dust and blush. She swirled on a peachy blush that held a fiery shimmer, focusing on the apples of her cheeks and sweeping up to the temples.

"*You're simply the best. Better than all the rest. Better than anyone I've ever met,*" she sang as she twirled around the room. If she repeated it enough, she might finally believe she was worthy of Anwar's love.

The psychic's warning rang in Lucy's mind almost as loud as the thumping music that filled her luxury suite.

"*In everyone's eyes, you are the Sheikh's forbidden bride. You must persuade him that your heart is strong, or there will be terrible consequences.*"

She had forgotten the prophecy, but now, the words assailed her on the eve of her exhibition.

And then Tina's words filled the room. "Give me a life-time of promises and a world of dreams. Speak a language of love like you know what it means."

Her love language was art. Her heart was filled with so much love and longing. She couldn't put the feelings into words as richly as she could in her art.

She glanced around her suite one last time and prayed that the friends and wealthy collectors Anwar had invited would perceive the love she had infused in her paintings and reward Anwar's belief in her in front of the crowd he had assembled.

CHAPTER THIRTY-SIX

W*as this even real?* Clutching the exhibition catalog to her chest, Lucy swept her gaze over the crowd gathered for the opening of the dazzling exhibition of her artworks created to honor the birth of her daughter, Rabah Minnie na Hassir.

She felt like pinching herself. Only six months ago, she had been in wintery New York, and now she was in the heat of the Arabian summer, surrounded by intoxicating works of art created from her heart. She swallowed a gulp of anxiety as Maria Bright approached the front of the room and began her address.

"With her ferocious beauty, breezy personality, and impressive artistic CV, it would've been easier to assume Lucy Ford had effortlessly made her way from obscurity, through the blinding lights of her sell-out exhibition in New York, to the present-day desert Kingdom of Avana, were it not for Anwar's endorsement," Maria said to the swelling crowd of exclusive attendees to her exhibition.

So far, so good, Lucy thought to herself. She had told Maria that she wanted to name the elephant in the room, the thought that may be impregnated in everyone's minds. She wanted to call it as she thought it, leaving no room for doubt. And Maria had agreed.

"However, anyone who assumes that this artistic tour de force has got to where she has on the back of the Sheikh's favoritism is doing her a grave disservice. Lucy has proven herself to be a tour de force of talent and grit, carving a niche that is hers alone. She weaves tears into smiles, produces mighty artistic statement pieces from her lithe, petite stature, and combusts detail with every flourish of her emotion-laden brush. Moreover, rather than run away from her heritage, she embraces her past and is abundantly proud of her roots."

Maria paused, reached for a glass of water, then took a slow, languid sip to add drama to her deliberate delay. "A fragmented family, parents who didn't love or encourage her, narcissistic siblings—Lucy learned at an early age to be self reliant."

Lucy's gaze drifted to the vast landscape she had painted running the length of the far wall. *Love Remembered.* Two words that healed her heart. Looking at the painting now, she thought how perfectly the name fitted. Anwar and she had never forgotten the love they once shared. Theirs was a love story of forgiveness and second chances.

Barely conscious of the crowd pressing around her, Lucy's heart quickened as she scanned the sensuous soft horizon, the vast, limitless expanse poured on the canvas with waves of deep sapphire blue, ochre, and gold. Her gaze honed in on the silhouette of a man and woman carrying a child infused within a thousand grains of sand. Her breath caught in her throat. It was so beautiful, full of emotion, and symbolic of everything she felt. The artwork had flowed through her as though created by an invisible force.

Maria's voice brought her back to the room. "'I will never

deny that having nothing made me fight harder,' Lucy has said. '"There were no gold-plated Lamborghinis parked in one of my gold-plated palaces, waiting to drive me to my gold-plated office. No permission to fail because Daddy guaranteed my fortune,'" she said, reading from the catalog.

A ripple of gentle laughter fluttered through the room. Through the sea of faces, Lucy noticed Anwar's younger brother, Fazza, grinning at her reference to his beloved Lamborghini. Beside him, Hamad stood with his arm encircled around a beautiful young woman.

Lucy sighed with relief. She had heeded the courage to call it as it was; people liked her authenticity and respected her honesty. And she had found it in her heart to forgive those who had wronged her—as they had found it in their hearts to forgive her.

It was a promising start.

CHAPTER THIRTY-SEVEN

The exhibition was a resounding success, attracting art enthusiasts worldwide. Critics praised the synergy between Lucy's evocative paintings and Sheikh Anwar's remarkable collection of emerging and established artists. Their partnership became the talk of the art world, an embodiment of passion, beauty, and creative synergy.

There were several highlights of the evening. To her amazement, Hamad used the event to publicly acknowledge how he had wronged Lucy and admitted his fault in purchasing the highly contentious painting *Salvator Mundi*. The painting subsequently disappeared, and all plans to exhibit it were abandoned. Finally, Lucy was free of the stain that had smeared her name and reputation.

People were excited to learn of Lucy's and Anwars' ambitious project, the *Maerid al'ahlam: The Gallery of Dreams*. Collectors couldn't wait to see what paintings were unveiled at the opening. Lucy and Anwar had decided it had to be a people's choice, and she was excited to see whose painting would adorn the massive entrance wall.

Yet, amid the success and acclaim, Lucy couldn't help but feel a sense of loss. Zephyr, the falcon that had accompanied them on their journey back to love and reminded them of their shared extraordinary connection, had vanished without a trace. His absence left a void in her heart.

Months passed, and Lucy continued to immerse herself in the art world, collaborating with renowned artists as she curated the museum's opening exhibition. Undoubtedly, Anwar and Lucy would challenge conventional boundaries and achieve their goal of uniting countries at war, but her thoughts often drifted to Zephyr. This falcon had guided her on this remarkable journey. During his absence, Anwar said very little, pouring his love and affection on their new bundle of joy, Princess Rabah. Along with Simba, the little lion she always carried, Anwar and she were inseparable.

It was on a relaxed autumn afternoon that fate intervened once again. As Lucy walked through the bustling local market, she caught sight of a familiar silhouette perched atop a vendor's cart. It was Zephyr, the fiercely protective and jealous pet falcon she had missed dearly.

With tears of joy streaming down her face, Lucy approached the vendor and pleaded for the falcon's return. The vendor, moved by her genuine emotion, agreed to part ways with Zephyr, recognizing their unbreakable bond.

"Anwar knows as well as I," he said, "A bird must always be free. He belongs to no one, but to the person he has given his heart."

Reunited with her feathered companion, Lucy felt a renewed sense of purpose. She knew that their journey together was far from over. With Zephyr by her side, she continued exploring the depths of artistic expression, seeking hidden treasures that could reshape perceptions and ignite the imagination. She embarked on a new collection of paintings, 'Flight of Passion.'

CHAPTER THIRTY-EIGHT

"Nicky Pelli is one of the most innovative young jewelers in the world," Hamad told Anwar as they entered her small studio. It was a bright, airy space filled with sketches, gemstones, and delicate pieces of jewelry adorning the walls and displays.

"There she is," he said, pointing to Nicky, a passionate and creative jewelry designer in her early thirties, who stood before a small group of aspiring designers, eager to hear her story.

Anwar recognized her from Lucy's exhibition. Clearly, she wasn't a passing fling, he thought as he watched Hamad, whose gaze never left her face.

"Good afternoon, everyone! Thank you for joining me today in my humble jewelry studio. I'm thrilled to have the opportunity to share with you why I became a jewelry designer and how one extraordinary woman, Elsa Peretti, inspired me on this journey."

On her studio wall, Nicky gestured towards a framed photograph of Elsa Peretti, an iconic Italian jewelry designer.

"Elsa Peretti is a name that resonates with elegance, innovation, and timeless beauty," Nicky said.

"Growing up, I was always drawn to art and fashion but never quite found my niche. It wasn't until I discovered Elsa's work that I felt a true connection to the world of jewelry design."

Nicky walked over to her workbench, where she kept a collection of Elsa Peretti-inspired pieces. "Elsa Peretti's designs are not just stunning; they uniquely capture emotions and tell a story. Her minimalist approach and emphasis on organic forms fascinated me from the moment I saw her work. I was captivated by the way she blended simplicity and sophistication effortlessly."

Nicky picked up a necklace adorned with a delicate silver heart pendant inspired by one of Elsa's famous creations. "This piece right here, inspired by Elsa's iconic Open Heart necklace, is a testament to her impact on my journey. It symbolizes love, vulnerability, and the power of connection. Through her designs, I discovered the true potential of jewelry—as not just an accessory but a means of self-expression and empowerment."

With a gentle touch, Nicky placed the necklace back on the display. "Elsa Peretti's influence goes beyond her designs. She was a trailblazer, a visionary woman who challenged the norms of the industry. Her collaboration with Tiffany & Co. brought her work to a wider audience, allowing her designs to become timeless classics."

Nicky walked back towards the group, her eyes filled with passion. "Inspired by Elsa's courage and creativity, I embarked on my own journey as a jewelry designer. I wanted to create pieces that evoked emotions, told stories, and empowered those who wore my designs. Jewellery can make us feel special, remind us of our inherent beauty and strength, and serve as a tangible reminder of life's precious moments."

Nicky paused, taking a moment to reflect. "I am standing before you today, sharing my story and passion for jewelry design. Elsa Peretti's influence will forever be etched in my heart, and I hope my creations can inspire others just as she inspired me."

Anwar and Hamad joined the audience in their applause, moved by Nicky's heartfelt story.

"Thank you all for joining me on this journey. I encourage you to find your own inspiration and muse and let your creativity shine. And remember, jewelry isn't just about the materials; it's about the stories we tell and the emotions we evoke."

With a final smile, Nicky bid farewell to her audience.

"I have approached her to design a capsule for my hotel and homewares line," Hamad said. "Our collaboration will be her first foray into homewares."

"I thought she was a jewelry designer." Anwar said as Nicky closed the door behind the departing students and placed a sign that read 'closed.'

"She is. But she is much more than that."

Anwar studied his brother's face. "You're quite obsessed with this Nicky Pelli, aren't you? Is that why you've brought me here?"

His brother grinned. "I have arranged a private viewing for you. I know you'll love her work. And I think Lucy will, too."

"Lucy?"

"You are going to do the romantic thing and get her an engagement ring, right?"

"We were married without the need to be engaged."

"Telling a woman she is marrying you and presenting her

with a contract to sign and actually proposing are two quite different things," he said, leading Anwar deeper into Nicky's studio. "Don't you want the real thing?"

"I have a sculptural approach for a designer," Nicky said, her face flushing as her sapphire-blue eyes locked with Hamad's. "Any piece I design has to be as beautiful when it's on the body as it does when it's on a surface."

Anwar noticed how his brother's gaze trailed over Nicky's body as though intimately familiar with her sensual curves.

She held Hamad's gaze and smiled, then gestured to her jewelry collection.

"They looked like miniature, gallery-worthy sculptures," Anwar said, his gaze drifting appreciatively over the rivulets etched in a broad band of gold. "Beautiful pieces of art."

"I don't view myself as an artist," Nicky said. "There's no message behind my work—it's more an expression of how I feel and want others to feel."

"You would get on very well with my wife Lucy. She's into feelings, too. She's an artist."

"I think of myself as a designer. I'm in a very mercantile world, which is quite different from being an artist," Nicky said. "But I appreciate the compliment. You're very kind. The ring you have been admiring is inspired by art. Architecture actually. And the desert. Along with the Italian designer Elsa Peretti, I'm inspired by many influences, including sculpture and photography, modernist furniture, and history. I like to think of my creations as modern artifacts for the curious mind."

"*You would definitely get on with my wife,*" Anwar laughed.

"This ring is inspired by how such artists have interacted with these natural formations and organic structures, reinterpreting them to express rhythm and movement in their work."

She passed the ring to Anwar and pointed to the repeating elements. "Rhythm denotes the repetition of visual elements such as line, shape, and color within space. A fundamental design principle, rhythm is essential for creating energy, movement, and emotion. This ring reinterprets nature's rhythms in unexpected ways. Asymmetric curves simulate the unfurling silhouettes of seashells. Ridges reference the transience of sand dunes, sculpted and dissolved by the wind. And tactile, sculptural proportions are softened by elegant gold, creating an object of sensual modernity. It's understated, elevated, and chic."

Hamad was right. Nicky and Lucy would get on fabulously. They were both passionate about creating things of meaning and beauty. And both were fiercely protective of their creative freedom.

"Your brother has been a great help to me," Nicky said. "I came for a short visit to Avana and stayed. I was quickly captivated by local artisans' artistry, skill, and dedication. It's largely thanks to Hamad that my design has evolved. I found a new respect for Arabic tradition and artisanship. I found my creative voice."

"Nicky has brought a personal and inimitable approach to jewelry design to our region," Hamad said. "Free from the constraints of formal training, she has honed a distinctive yet refined style. She has gained creative recognition and professional esteem within the industry. She is as uncompromising about resolutely sustainable design, ethics, and kindness as she is dedicated to honoring the individuality of the discerning woman. Most importantly, she is committed to telling their stories – their passions, quirks, and joys – through her jewelry."

"Now, with Hamad's backing, I can spread my wings," she said, gesturing to three limited-edition candelabras in bronze, silver, and gold, which decorated the studio. "I was quite free to design for me before, but Hamad asked for different proportions—giant proportions. From small to spectacular," she said with a laugh. "I set myself a personal design challenge to ensure that each candelabra can be positioned in two different ways: "You flip one of them 90 degrees and the other two 180 degrees to give them a different look. I like the versatility and playful aspect."

"Play and passion," Anwar said. "Lucy's core values."

His brother was right. A customized engagement ring by Nicky would be just the symbol of the true love his marriage deserved—classically timeless but with a modern twist.

"Can you design something truly bespoke? An exceptional ring for an exceptional person on a very special day?" he asked.

Nicky nodded. "Of course. It would be my pleasure."

CHAPTER THIRTY-NINE

A nwar had been planning this moment for months, wanting to make it as unique and unforgettable as their love story. He knew that Lucy deserved nothing less than sheer perfection. With the help of the renowned jewelry powerhouse Nicky Pelli, he designed an engagement ring that embodied their unique bond and celebrated Lucy's artistic spirit.

On a picturesque afternoon, Anwar walked with Lucy through a secluded garden adorned with blooming orchids and a serene waterfall. The air was filled with the sweet scent of jasmine, adding a touch of romance to the already magical ambiance. As they strolled hand in hand, sensing something extraordinary was about to unfold, Lucy's heart fluttered with curiosity and excitement.

Anwar led her to an elegant table under a canopy of date trees adorned with delicate china and crystal glasses, reflecting the sunlight like precious gems. As they took their seats, Lucy couldn't help but notice a small, intricately wrapped gift box in front of her. Her eyes widened, a surge of anticipation coursing through her veins.

With a sparkle in his eyes, Anwar leaned forward, his voice filled with love and adoration. "Lucy, my dearest heart, from the first day our paths crossed, you have inspired me and awakened a passion within my soul. You are my muse, the light that brightens my every day."

He reached across the table, his hand trembling slightly, and gently placed the gift box in Lucy's hands. Her heart raced as she carefully untied the rose-pink bow, her fingers trembling with excitement. She lifted the lid slowly, revealing a breathtaking engagement ring beautifully crafted by Nicky Pelli. The centerpiece was a giant pink sapphire, which shone with extraordinary brilliance.

Lucy's eyes widened with wonder as she beheld the exquisite design.

"I know Nicky Pelli's work. I've seen her in Arab Vogue. She's one of the brightest, most innovative stars in jewelry design," Lucy said, gazing at the beautiful gift. "It couldn't be more perfect."

The ring showcased a mesmerizing piece of art, an ethereal fusion of delicate diamonds sweeping around the central sapphire and intricate sweeps of gold. Delicate arabesque patterns were meticulously engraved around the sides of the ring, adding an extra touch of splendor and uniqueness to the already extraordinary piece.

Tears welled in her eyes; It was as if Nicky had captured the essence of their relationship and transformed it into a tangible symbol of their love. Lucy looked up at Anwar, her voice filled with emotion. "Anwar, this ring... It's exquisite. I can't believe you've created something so incredibly beautiful and unique for me. You didn't have to. I didn't need you to buy me an expensive ring to know how you feel."

Anwar smiled, his eyes gleaming with love. "I wanted to, *habibti*. This ring represents the beauty of our love, the strength of our devotion, and the promise of our future together. Will you paint the canvas of our lives with your extraordinary talent as my partner, soulmate, and forever love? Will you do me the honor of becoming my wife? "

"But I am already your wife," she whispered.

"You were my reluctant bride. The wife I stole and sought to tame. I never asked for your hand in marriage. I demanded it. I disrespected you. We must love each other so that the person we care for with all our hearts feels truly loved," Anwar said. "You have given that to me in spades, including the portrait of Zephyr and, of course, the birth of our daughter. The ring Nicky created for you is inspired by the orchid-shaped architecture of my brother's wife Melanie and the *Shutfah*, a traditional headpiece worn by kings, leaders, and influential men. I told Nicky to design for a strong, empowered woman—not a woman stolen by a sheikh."

Anwar rose from the table, then knelt on one knee at her feet. "Lucy, will you do me the honor of marrying and loving me freely as my untamed bride?"

Lucy's heart soared, overwhelmed by a wave of love and joy. She nodded, her voice choked with emotion. "Yes, Anwar, three thousand and three times yes!"

With trembling hands, Anwar gently took the ring from the box and slipped it onto Lucy's finger. "Now we have a wedding to plan. In Paris, the city of love."

The world around them seemed to fade away as they shared a tender, passionate kiss, sealing their commitment.

In that magical moment, as they held each other, surrounded by the beauty of nature and the promise of forever, Anwar and Lucy knew that their love story would continue to unfold, each chapter filled with breathtaking moments, just like this one.

CHAPTER FORTY

"You told me you loved Leonardo's painting more than any other. And so, my love, I thought, how best to give you the fairytale wedding you always dreamed of."

Lucy stood in the Denon Wing in the Louvre in front of the portrait of Mona Lisa, tears filling her eyes, as Anwar slipped a gold band engraved with delicate arabesque patterns on her finger.

Surrounded by exquisite artworks and their closest friends and family who gathered to witness the magical moment, the gallery was filled with beauty and love. Anwar looked so distinguished and regal dressed in traditional Arabic attire, alongside Lucy, radiant and elegant in her white lace wedding gown.

Soft, ethereal music fluttered over them as their eyes met, and a wave of love and joy washed over them. *The Mona Lisa*, the enigmatic masterpiece, hanging on the wall behind the couple, seemingly following their every move. A bed of exotic pink orchids carpeted the floor, adding a touch of enchantment to the scene.

"I thought you didn't believe in Valentine's Day," Lucy whispered, referencing their wedding date.

"I don't. But you do, and that's all that matters," he nodded to his brother Fazza, who stepped forward and handed Anwar a small gift box of handmade French chocolates tied with a silk red bow. He leaned down and presented them to two-year-old Rabah. "For you, my princess, happy Valentine's Day."

He turned to Lucy and whispered, "We don't want our daughter to feel *love-starved*, do we?"

"Oh, Anwar, you remembered."

"I have never forgotten the things that speak to your heart, *habibti.* "

Lucy spun around the gallery, registering the look of deep love and acceptance on everyone's faces, then glanced toward the painting. It embodied many things important to her and Leonardo—beauty, mystery, and enduring love. She would never understand the mysterious forces that had brought Anwar and her together, but she knew that finally, after so much pain and heartache, she had found everlasting love.

"Our love is a work of art. Just like Leonardo's painting. An eternal masterpiece that will endure through the ages," Anwar said as though reading her thoughts.

"It's a dream come true," she whispered. She saw her happy heart reflected as she stared into his golden eyes. "I am honored to be your bride, wife, and mother to our daughter," she said, drawing Rabah, their little flower girl, to her side. "And to embark on this journey of love, passion, and creativity with you both."

The guests watched in awe, captivated by the love and devotion emanating from the couple as they laced their hands together, their eyes locked in a profound connection.

"In the presence of this masterpiece, we gather to witness

the union of Sheikh Anwar Na Hassir and his artist bride, Lucy," the marriage celebrant said in a deep, official voice. "May your love be as enduring as the strokes of paint on Leonardo's artwork, and may your love inspire others to seek beauty and love in their lives."

As he proceeded with the wedding ceremony, their words echoed through the gallery. They exchanged heartfelt vows, promising to support and uplift each other in their creative and philanthropic endeavors.

Anwar and Lucy shared their first kiss as a happily married couple, sealing their enduring love in front of the iconic Mona Lisa.

If Lucy was any happier, she thought her heart might crack. "*Ahwa, habibti. Ahwa, habibti. Ahwa, habibti,*" she repeated. "I am in love—to infinity and back.'

Her stomach fluttered as Anwar bent and kissed her again.

"I'm pregnant, my love," she whispered. "We're having another baby!"

"We gave love a second chance," he cried, turning to their family and friends. "And we've won the lottery!"

"To love!" Lucy said, throwing her bouquet in the air.

Cries of joy echoed through the gallery as Hamad's girl-friend, Nicky Pelli, caught the bouquet. Lucy turned to Mona Lisa's portrait. Her dark, exotic eyes appeared to brighten, and her soft carmine lips curved into a happy smile.

You wanted to feel forever love, the portrait seemed to whisper, *and now you've found it.*

EPILOGUE

S even years and three beautiful children later, twin boys and another daughter, the construction of *Maerid al'ahlam: The Gallery of Dreams* neared completion. Lucy and Anwar had poured their hearts and souls into this project, and soon, their vision would be unveiled to the world. The global anticipation was palpable, and word of the collection spread like sunlight, igniting curiosity and sparking conversations about why women's artistic genius had slumbered in darkness for so long.

On the day of the grand opening, Anwar stood outside the museum before a crowd of media, art enthusiasts, dignitaries, and women artists from across the globe. His speech echoed with passion and hope as he expressed his gratitude for the unwavering support he had received throughout the transformative journey from dream to reality.

As Anwar cut the expansive silk ribbon draped over the doors of *Maerid al'ahlam: The Gallery of Dreams,* they swung open, revealing a world where women's artistic contributions took center stage. Anwar registered Lucy's shocked surprise when she saw her painting, *Desert Dreams,* and

Healing is Possible, gracing the entrance walls alongside the world's most famous painting loaned from The Louvre for the opening—The Mona Lisa.

"Our people were unanimous," Anwar said. "When asked to vote for the pieces they most wanted to see honored, your work was right up there with Leonardo's portrait. They loved your powerful narratives of hope, love, and forgiveness."

The museum quickly became a cultural landmark, attracting art lovers from every corner of the world. Lucy and Anwar knew that there were three cornerstones to the success of *Maerid al'ahlam*. The spectacular architecture designed by Melanie, the richness of its permanent collection (thanks to loans from the Louvre and other French museums), and the quality of its temporary exhibitions, rich with diverse cultural perspectives.

Anwar's and Lucy's ambitions had been realized. The Gallery of Dreams stood as a testament to their vision, unwavering belief in art's healing power, and the importance of celebrating women artists. Leonardo was a renowned supporter of women's rights to be treated equally, and his portrait of Lisa powerfully symbolized everything *Maerid al'ahlam* stood for.

The collection will inspire generations to come and shine a light on the immense talent that has been overlooked for far too long.

As Anwar and Lucy walked through the museum, observing the joy and wonder on visitors' faces, he turned to Lucy.

"The Gallery of Dreams has become a world-class museum and a symbol of empowerment. It will always be a reminder when women's artistic contributions are celebrated rather than suppressed, we enrich our collective cultural heritage," Anwar said. "I have you to thank for that."

"We have each other to thank," she said. "Our love has enriched our lives and created a legacy."

"I'm immensely proud of what we've achieved, and I'm immensely proud of you," he said. "You've left an indelible mark on the art world and inspired countless artists to dream big and create fearlessly."

"We felt the fear and loved anyway, didn't we, Anwar?"

"Yes, *habibti,* we did."

"Anwar—"

'Yes, my love?"

"Did I ever tell you that I'm glad my heart was stolen by the sheikh?"

"No, I don't think you did," he laughed. "Why don't we go to bed and indulge our blessings—of which there are plenty."

* * * THE END * * *

Happily, peace prevailed as previously antagonistic neighboring countries bent their will to the prosperity of all and followed the lead of Lucy and Anwar's vision of heaven on earth.

THE AUDIO AND PAPERBACK VERSION OF *STOLEN BY THE SHEIKH* IS ALSO AVAILABLE NOW.

AUTHOR'S NOTE

Dear readers,

Like so many of my stories, *Stolen by The Sheikh* explores many of the issues that are important to me.

It's a very distressing truth that a significant number of beautiful, kind souls have suffered because of the hurtful behaviour of family members who are suffering from Narcissistic Disorder Syndrome.

One definition from <u>The Mayo Clinic</u> is as follows:

> *Narcissistic personality disorder is a mental health condition in which people have an unreasonably high sense of their own importance. They need and seek too much attention and want people to admire them. People with this disorder may lack the ability to understand or care about the feelings of others.*

Some people have suggested that as many as 50 per cent of the Western population may be afflicted. We certainly seem to live in an era where the golden rule that I grew up with, "Do unto others as you would have them do unto you," has been lost on so many.

But then, when we look a little deeper, it seems that the people who are doing the hurting have been wounded in their childhoods. And so the trauma cycle repeats.

Unfortunately, people with all the hallmarks of Narcissistic Disorder Syndrome are seldom clinically diagnosed and rarely seek treatment. Instead, mothers, fathers, brothers, sisters, husbands and wives—people from all walks of life operate from a lens of envy and take pleasure in stealing people's happiness and making people feel sad.

I wanted to explore this issue in *Stolen By The Sheikh* and show how self-love, compassion, empowerment through education, and true unconditional love can and do work miracles on the journey to healing for those who have been mistreated so unfairly.

It's heartbreaking not to be loved by your mother and to have hateful lies spread about you—as you'll discover in Lucy's story. But art brings healing—as does faith and the love of Sheikh Anwar na Hassir.

I hope you enjoyed Anwar's and Lucy's story.

ACKNOWLEDGMENTS

I am indebted and forever grateful to my beautiful BETA and ARC readers. I would like to acknowledge and say a special thanks to Sharon Abrams. Her early review, the first, broke my anxiety barrier and made me smile. A heartfelt thank you.

Next, Renee Ferritto. You always come through with an acute ability to pick up those pesky typos. It doesn't matter how often I read the text aloud or use tools like Grammarly, you are adept at picking things up! Thank you!

And Mary Lou, for your kind words and for picking up a few sneaky typos that still crept through!

DM if you would like to join my team of passionate BETA and ARC readers and journey together in the books of love and happily ever afters.

MEET THE CAST OF CHARACTERS

Passionate, wounded, and hopelessly romantic, the na Hassirs are a family you won't forget!

ANWAR, MELANIE AND TARIQ.

If you haven't read <u>Claimed by the Sheikh</u>, you'll enjoy meeting the characters who also take more of a starring role in the second book in the series—Anwar, Melanie and Tariq.

You'll find more details here: https://www.molliemath ews.com/claimed-by-the-sheikh/

Read to the end for a bonus excerpt

ISSY RILEY, THE ART THERAPIST

Did you enjoy meeting Issy Riley, the art therapist who had encouraged Lucy to paint? Read Issy and Massimilliano Balforni's love story in <u>The Italian Billionaire's Christmas Bride</u>

. . .

Billionaire business magnate, Gianni Romano ventured to New Zealand driven by the crimes of his father and the memories he wants to escape. When he bumps into flame-haired siren Kate Millar, the spark they have is hotter than a Sicilian sunset and conflict flames. When emotions run deep and hearts are on the line, will mixing business with pleasure be the bedrock for a lifelong love? Or will their love explode like an angry volcano?

KATE AND GIANNI

Read Kate and Gianni's love story, in *Love All of Me.*

What if you hate Christmas and along comes a red hot Italian Billionaire Santa?

After surviving a horrific accident last Christmas, Kate Miller is plagued by guilt. Hiding both her mental and physical scars, she shuns love and escapes into work—finding meaning and purpose in running her global manuka honey empire.

Beautiful and intelligent, her passions are inflamed when Gianni Romano demands she sell the business to him. How dare he think he can buy the only thing that gives her a reason to live?

Love All of Me is a Christmas romance novel blazing with the promise of a happily ever after. Set in Sicily, Italy, and The Bay of Islands, New Zealand—two of the world's most beautiful, unspoiled, sensuous places.

"Another heart-wrenching yet heart-healing story from this gifted author…"

MARIA BRIGHT

Maria Bright, the gallery owner and Anwar's new art adviser, makes a star appearance in the award-winning romance Love in Venice. When two hopelessly mismatched people share a love for art, a passion for love, and a city like Venice, nothing is truly impossible…or is it? You'll find all the links and a preview here: Love in Venice.

 "I loved this story! *Love In Venice* leans toward the heart. Where love is the main character. Where you cheer for their relationship to flourish. There is one thing wrong with the story…I never wanted it to end. Honestly, I've never felt this way about a story before. ENJOY!"

~ **Jan Z.**

DON'T MISS THE NEXT BOOK (OR OTHER BOOKS) IN THE SERIES!

For news on upcoming books, sign up for Mollie Mathew's New Release Newsletter (and receive a free eBook): http://eepurl.com/ghM501

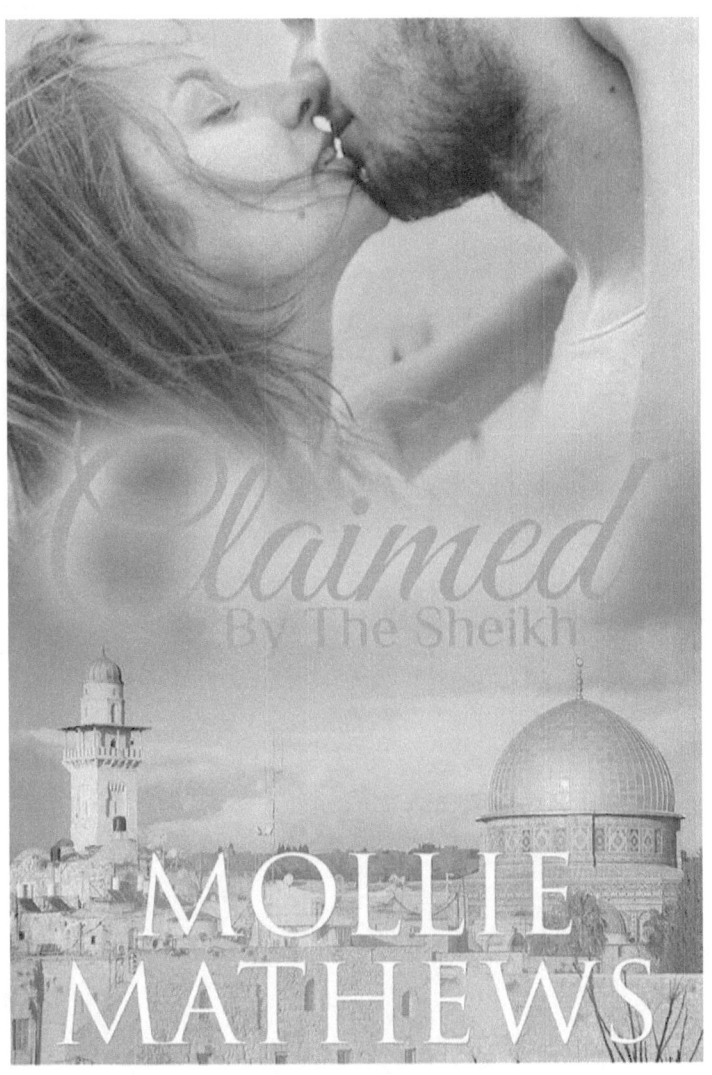

CLAIMED BY THE SHEIKH EXCERPT

I hope you enjoyed reading about Anwar's older brother Sheikh Tariq na Hassir. If you did, you'll enjoy his love story.

Read on for a free excerpt of this full-length romance, Claimed by The Sheikh.

The secret she kept from the Sheikh...

ABOUT THIS LOVE STORY

A grief-stricken Sheikh Tariq na Hassir, the formidable ruler of the Kingdom of Avana, arrives in Paris to claim his brother's child after a car crash killed his parents--unaware that the child isn't their biological son. Salim is Tariq's son, with his former lover, a renowned architect.

Three years ago, after being banished by Tariq from his desert kingdom, Melanie Jones secretly gave her baby to Tariq's childless brother and his wife, in a swap the world was never supposed to discover.

The tragedy pulls her back to the world that rejected her and the man who abandoned her—the only man capable of turning her carefully controlled world upside down.

Tariq will do whatever it takes to protect his legacy, including claiming Melanie as his bride and his son as heir.

But Melanie has other plans for her future—a westernized life where she's free to operate her own business, control her own life, and meet a man who loves her for who she is.

"A magical, mystical, hauntingly beautiful story which will stay with you forever."

EXCERPT

"Are you trying to kill her?" Tariq na Hassir, the formidable ruler of the Kingdom of Avana, seized the animal handler's arm, forcing him to release the rope laced around the baby giraffe's neck.

"She has suffered enough trauma." Tariq dismissed the man with a fierce scowl that struck fear into enemies.

A slither of panic crept into the young man's hushed apology. "I am sorry your Excellency."

"Release the others from their cages," Tariq growled.

The man did not have to be asked twice. He knew from experience that the Sheikh's retribution for disobedience would be swift and merciless.

"You are safe from harm," Tariq said softly, stroking the baby giraffe's long neck with a gentleness that belied his strength.

"No one will ever hurt you again, Noor," he said softly, impulsively naming her as his fingertips swept through the calf's fur. He let his long supple fingers linger a moment upon her tail. Thankfully they had saved her in time, he thought as he reached for the reins, clenching his powerful hands around the soft leather.

The rage he had first felt on hearing about the ruthless murder of the new born's mother still roared through him. Had she been executed to pay a tail dowry to the father of some money-mongering bride, he wondered? Or did some heinous person pay thousands of dollars for a wretched fly swatter?

Noor looked up and met Tariq's dark gaze. In her innocent eyes, he saw her despair, her disillusionment, her disgust with humanity. He recognised her trauma as though it was his own. Because it was.

"Humans," he said, his voice marinated with contempt. "The people you should be able to trust, the people who say they care, the people whose actions should be driven by love —the majority are driven by nothing but selfishness, deception, and lies."

Taking a bottle of milk, he placed the teat to Noor's lips. The calf's silky black lashes grazed her cheeks as she gazed down at the foreign object then looked back at Tariq. She stared silently up at him, her eyes moist and bewildered.

Tariq had trained himself to shut down his emotions but that skill suddenly failed him. His chest trembled with suppressed rage knowing the orphaned baby would never again taste her mother's milk.

"What passes for love among some people is abhorrent," he said in a low, strained voice. "On behalf of humanity, I apologise."

The killing of the calf 's mother and three other rare Kordofan giraffes by trophy hunters seeking their tails further motivated the Sheikh's commitment to transform his anger into action.

"Do you really think you can save her?"

Tariq looked at Anwar, his younger brother by 11 months. His head was slightly bowed but he could see his eyes were fixed in sadness and longing.

Tension ripped down Tariq's spine. "Our father's reign of terror and tyranny have robbed Avana of prosperity and peace. I will make it my personal mission to right the injustices of the past. War and hostility must end. And it starts with how we treat those most vulnerable."

His fingers shook as he gripped the bottle of milk as Noor, at last, began to suckle.

An eerie silence swept across the precipitous landscape of Avana's Tiwa oasis. Tariq lifted his gaze to the horizon. The only movement visible to his naked eye was the wind etching a delicate furrow as it crawled over the golden dunes.

"Not only will I provide a sanctuary for hunted wildlife and orphans like Noor, but I will liberate God's most precious creatures from the many closing zoos and other inhumane habitats around the world," he glanced over at the other animals being unloaded from the custom-built crates.

"I will create a world-acclaimed sanctuary, impenetrable by those with impure and malicious hearts. It will be the most magical, marvellous, mesmerisingly unique place, the number one eco-tourism destination in the world. I will create meaningful employment for our people, restoring their dignity, attracting millions of visitors annually and contributing billions to the economy. But more importantly, I will show the world how kindness and compassion can be turned into plutonium and change the world."

Anwar glanced at the now lush landscape and recalled how barren it had once been. With no sign of life in sight, others had found it impossible to fathom his brother's vision to transform the punishing and unforgiving conditions into a haven for so many endangered species. Yet, as with everything Tariq turned his formidable will and mind-blowing wealth to, he had succeeded where mere mortals were destined to fail.

Anwar's heart swelled with pride as he thought of all his brother's achievements. "It's an audacious and admirable plan. And if anyone can pull it off it's you, brother. Your passion, your drive, your unrelenting ambition and pursuit of goals exceeds mere mortals. And you have the endurance and power of 13,000 Arabian horses, but aren't you setting yourself up for too much hard work? Why don't you relax? Kick back. Enjoy the fruits of your reign?" Anwar said, tossing his head in the direction of the harem. "Other men would."

"Women were our father's weakness," bitterness bled from his words. "I too once made the same mistake. I too paid the price."

There was a tense silence while Tariq lifted his gaze to the sky and studied the giant falcon circling above.

"Was it not you who once taught that your greatest weakness can also be your greatest strength?" Anwar asked.

Tariq shook his head, biting down a terse retort. "I was misled." He said, nodding his command to the animal handler lingering at a respectful distance.

He petted Noor as she was led away. "All kinds of atrocities are committed in the name of love, which is why it is the most dangerous of emotions, and why I am forever turned off to women."

Let Claimed by The Sheikh take you away from it all…
the *Sheikhs Untamed Brides* series, where love always gets a second chance.

Available now!

Claimed by the Sheikh (Tariq and Melanie)
Stolen By The Sheikh (Anwar and Lucy)
Bought By The Sheikh (Fazza and Grace)

EXCERPT: BOUGHT BY THE SHEIKH

ABOUT THIS LOVE STORY

Sometimes, love is the greatest ride of all.

In the opulent and enchanting world of Arabian royalty, 31-year-old charismatic playboy, Sheikh Prince Fazza na Hassir finds himself face-to-face with a challenge that will test his business acumen and his heart. When he sets his formidable business skills on acquiring the prestigious Ferrari company, little does he know that his life is about to collide with that of an extraordinary American woman.

Grace Hunt, a fiercely independent and brilliant CEO, has moved to Aibud to escape from her toxic family. Dedicating her life to revolutionizing the automobile industry, when she learns that a captivating Arabian prince wishes to acquire her beloved Ferrari brand, she is determined to resist his charms and protect her legacy.

Known for his wealth, power, and insatiable desire for beauty, things take a turn for the worse when Fazza tries to buy her affection. But Grace is not a woman who can be bought by the sheikh.

Bought By The Sheikh weaves a mesmerizing tale of love,

passion, and destiny, set against the backdrop of opulent Arabian palaces and the thrilling world of luxury automobiles. Escape into a world where love knows no boundaries and where two souls, seemingly worlds apart, find solace and strength in each other.

Defying the odds and rewriting their destinies, *Bought By The Sheikh* reminds us that freedom is not worth having if it does not include the freedom to make mistakes and that sometimes, unconditional love is the greatest freedom of all.

A compelling and thrilling story about a powerful woman and her equally formidable opponent

EXCERPT

My whole life is a lie.

Grace Hunt fought back tears as she watched the video testimonial clients had posted on YouTube. The words slid over her like a contaminated slick of oil over the pristine waters of the Arabian Sea as she listened to the praise they lavished upon her. "Grace is a wonderful person." "Grace has changed our lives."

The testimonials should fuel her, but now, thanks to the damage her family had wrought, she felt dead to kind words. How could she believe anything anyone said anymore?

How could her family have betrayed her so brutally? How could her mother say such shockingly unkind things when she was alive? How could her brother and sister have stolen her inheritance? When she had been so good and kind and loving to them all. How had she become the scapegoat for her family's dysfunction?

Jealousy.

Wasn't that what the therapist had said? "They're jealous. No," she had corrected. "They're envious. Envy seeks to destroy."

"Families are meant to love," Grace had protested—naïvely, as it turned out.

"Sometimes there's nothing worse than family," the therapist had said.

Grace shut the laptop and walked to the panoramic windows of her penthouse apartment overlooking the glittering skyscrapers of Dubai. Tears fell down her cheeks. A month ago, she had had a loving family. At least, she had convinced herself she did. Now, she had ousted their lies. There was no going back. She had been a sister, a daughter, an aunt, and a cousin. But now she had no one. She was alone again.

Indefinitely.

There had been no other option but to walk away after the scandal erupted. Fly away, she corrected, gazing out at the Arabian landscape that months ago had been so foreign to her. Was she destined always to be an outsider, she wondered? An imposter? A stranger—even to those she loved?

She wasn't even an envious person. She wanted the best for everyone. But in the end, it didn't matter. She was the sacrificial lamb in their ravenous hunger for slaughter. It didn't have to be like this, she mused. They had made their choice when they had hidden the truth from her last Christmas until she had no choice but to confront the facts.

They hated her. Hated her beauty. Hated her popularity. Hated her goodness. Hated the success she had worked so bloody hard to achieve. She was a modern-day Cinderella, living a nightmare. There was no prince riding to her rescue. No handsome Middle-Eastern ruler to kiss away her tears. No desert warrior ready to battle her assailants.

No one to hold her.

A salty tear trickled down her lips. She wiped it away and vowed it would be her last.

Dubai, known for its luxury shopping, ultramodern architecture and lively nightlife, suited Grace and her thirst for escape perfectly. No one could blame her for not wanting to return to New York, she mused as she looked around her penthouse apartment decorated with modern artworks by contemporary Islamic artists. Her eyes lingered over the painting she had purchased that night, *Ya Kalbi.*

Lucy Ford was a contemporary New York artist who now called the Middle East home. Her latest collection was heavily influenced by her new home and love of Islamic architecture. Marrying into the Royal Family had obviously fueled her creativity, Grace thought with admiration. She admired people who found true love in foreign places, avoiding worn cliches of Internet dating, short-term flings, and even shorter marriages.

Grace loved her new works and knew she had to purchase *Ya Kalbi* instantly. The English translation meant *My Heart*, but she preferred the romantic, lyrical feel of the words spoken in Arabic. It was love at first sight, she mused, as her gaze traveled across her new acquisition.

As she savoured the wash of emerald greens gliding across a sea of gold, an image of the audaciously opulent Lamborghini arriving at Lucy's exhibition and the green-eyed desert prince emerging from it flashed in her mind. An unwelcome kick of desire rose within her now, as it had then. The sheikh obviously needed educating on the superiority of Ferrari, she affirmed, bending her will toward the sole focus of her life.

Her career.

What an incredible coup it would be, she decided, to covert the royal ruler.

"What do you do when, your whole life, you've been told you're a failure?" She had asked her therapist before leaving New York.

"You succeed," she had replied. "Only you redefine success."

"How?"

"What does success mean to your family?"

"Stealing," Grace had said unhesitatingly. "Extracting money by any means. Thieving, even from those you love. Oh, and then there are the lies. Success means being an accomplished liar. Lying is a sport. Who could get what, from who, at any cost—and get away with it."

"I wasn't selfish enough," Grace had said truthfully.

"So, you were sacrificed."

"The irony was that my mother limited me by telling me that I was, in fact, *too selfish*, *too in love with myself*, that I needed to play small so my siblings could shine."

"Why?"

"I have no idea. It's not like we're a royal dynasty needing preserving."

"Gaslighting," the therapist said. "It's classic, covert, narcissistic manipulation."

* * *

Grace thought of these things the following evening as she stood poised on stage, prepared to unveil the newest, most pioneering, legendary Ferrari. The ballroom of the Dubai Hilton room hummed with anticipation. The utterly original design had been kept top secret, and tonight, Enzo Ferrari's pioneering spirit of innovation would take centre stage.

Throughout her career, she had cultivated relationships

with nearly all the richest men in the world. Grace prided herself on her rare achievement of never sleeping with any of them on her rise to the top. It wasn't through want of their trying.

Amongst the audience she hoped would attend tonight was one man she had never succeeded in seducing. The elusive Playboy prince she had glimpsed at the opening of Lucy's Ford's exhibition. *Sheikh Fazzaz na Hassir*. He was wedded exclusively to Lamborghini.

Lamborghini's shameless marketing tactics included lusty, surgically-enhanced blondes with fewer scruples than a bitch on heat.

Invited for the most exclusive revelation the supercar world had ever offered, only the wealthiest, most astute collectors were gathered. She searched for her target, shielding her eyes from the bright spotlights illuminating the stage. Had she succeeded? Would Sheikh Fazzaz na Hassir come? His love of Lamborghinis was purportedly unshake-able, her intel had told her that. As they had his voracious conquests of the women who sold them. What he wanted. He got. He called the shots. *Always.*

She stood on the stage, fully aware that by adhering to the dress code of the Middle East of almost monastic proprietary, she was employing the most subtle, tantalisingly aphrodisiac tool she had at her disposal. The cream silk Lanvin dress clung to her Marilyn Monroe curves and clinched waist, falling to just above her calves, showcasing her narrow ankles. Rather than concealing her beauty, the high neckline majestically spotlighted her delicate face and statement lips, skilfully accented in a luscious shade of Ferrari red for maximum impact. Her green eyes, she knew, smoked and smouldered even from a distance, with chic winged eyes creating a strong but feminine vibe. As she surveyed the crowd, she ran her hand over her sleek black hair, gently touching the long locks caught in a sophisticated knot at the nape of her neck.

Her whole look was artfully curated to give her the exotic look she knew drove men wild. She wouldn't sleep her way to sales, but she knew beauty that was hard to get was a winning strategy. Playboys, billionaires and Sheikhs loved the rare, the desirable, the elusive—and the unattainable. It was a formula for success that she would not be breaking.

Her eyes fell upon Lucy Ford and her husband, Sheikh Anwar na Hassir, then sank disappointedly. The seat next to him was empty. While not a condition of Grace purchasing her painting, Lucy had promised to do her best to ensure her brother-in-law's attendance. Perhaps he had been delayed, she hoped, summoning more optimism than she felt. Had she misjudged his appetite for beautiful, elusive women when she had ignored him at the opening?

She had staked her reputation on her ability to force the defection of Fazzaz na Hassir from Lamborghini. She took a slow, languid sip of sparkling water and tried to buy time. Still, he did not appear. She couldn't delay any longer. She knew time equated with money in the agendas of those gathered. The hand of success or failure rose or fell on her punctuality.

"Your Royal Highness', esteemed guests, thank you for your attendance tonight," she began. "Ferrari is pleased to announce the most innovative, audacious, and ground-breaking release in the history of supercars."

She nodded toward the side of the stage, silently directing that the floor-length silk curtains concealing the new design be drawn back. She kept her eyes on the audience, wanting to witness their reaction when they saw the Ferrari XTC888 GTB for the first time.

The look of astonished bewilderment was not what she was expecting. Her gut churned as she turned. She sucked in a deep, ragged breath. "What the f—"

The stage was empty.

The priceless Ferrari was gone!

Let <u>Bought By The Sheikh</u> take you on a wild ride to love... the *Sheikhs Untamed Brides* series, where love always gets a second chance.

Pre-order now!

5-STAR ADVANCE REVIEWS

"Readers who love sheikdom stories will love this one with its familiar trope."

"Great story and world-building as I never read a Sheikh book before, so it leaves me wanting to know more about Grace and Amir's story."

ABOUT THE AUTHOR

MOLLIE MATHEWS is a New Zealand author who writes fun, sophisticated, passion-filled contemporary romance. She is known for her "sensual, beautiful, empowered stories enveloped in true romance" (5-star review). Her books have resonated with a global audience. She has been featured in magazines, television, and radio.

A former child and family therapist Mollie passionately believes in the power of romance to transform people's lives. She loves Mother Theresa's words, *"We are all pens in the hands of a writing God sending love letters to the world."*

Her stories are unashamedly positive, optimistic, full of fun and passion.

She is graduate of Victoria University, in Wellington, New Zealand and has given keynote speeches at romance writers conventions and international seminars.

Mollie follows the sun, dividing her time between New Zealand and exotic locations—wherever she intends setting her next romance novel. She lives with her very own romantic hero, Lorenzo—tall, dark, terribly handsome and fluent in Spanish!

Follow Mollie on BookBub https://www.bookbub.com/authors/mollie-mathews

Be inspired by Mollie on Instagram www.instagram.com/molliemathewsauthor

Follow Mollie on TikTok www.tiktok.com/@molliewritesromance

Join Mollie's Readers Group on Facebook at https://www.facebook.com/groups/323525616931811

Or follow www.facebook.com/molliemathewsnz

Check out her inspiration board on Pinterest www. nz.pinterest.com/molliemathews/

BY MOLLIE MATHEWS

THE SHEIKHS UNTAMED BRIDES

CLAIMED BY THE SHEIKH
STOLEN BY THE SHEIKH
BOUGHT BY THE SHEIKH (Coming Soon)

GEMSTONE BILLIONAIRES

THE ITALIAN BILLIONAIRE'S CHRISTMAS BRIDE
THE ITALIAN BILLIONAIRE'S SCANDALOUS
MARRIAGE
GEMSTONE BILLIONAIRES 2 BOOK-BUNDLE
BOX SET
GEMSTONE BILLIONAIRES 3 BOOK-BUNDLE
BOX SET

TRUE LOVE

LOVE IN VENICE (3rd place winner Koru Award)
LOVE IN MEXICO

LOVE IN MONTANA (Coming Soon)

PASSION DOWN UNDER SASSY SHORT STORIES

FINDING A HUSBAND
TWIST OF FATE
LOVE ME FOREVER
LOVE ME AS I AM
FOREVER AND ALWAYS
THE LIGHTKEEPER'S LOVER
PASSION DOWN UNDER 2 BOOK-BUNDLE BOX SET
(Books 1 & 2)
PASSION DOWN UNDER 3 BOOK-BUNDLE BOX SET
(Books 1, 2 & 3)

ISBN eBook: 978-1-99-105309-1

ISBN print: 978-1-99-105310-7

ISBN print D2D: 978-1-99-105318-3

Cover Design: © Steven Novak

Published by

Blue Orchid Publishing New Zealand

Blue Orchid
PUBLISHING

Visit www.molliemathews.com to read more about all our books and to buy them. You will also find features, author interviews, and news of author events, and you can sign up for e-newsletters so that you're always first to hear about our new releases.